Reading Power 系列

Intermediate

★ 中級全民英檢必備
★ 學科能力測驗／指定科目考試／統一入學測驗必備

Intermediate Reading ④
新聞宅急通

三民英語編輯小組　彙編

ACKNOWLEDGEMENT

The articles in this publication are adapted from the works by Theodore J. Pigott and Jason W. Crockett.

三民書局

國家圖書館出版品預行編目資料

Intermediate Reading 4:新聞宅急通 B／三民英語編輯
小組彙編.－－初版五刷.－－臺北市：三民，2018
面；　　公分.－－(Reading Power系列)
含索引
ISBN 978–957–14–5178–7　(平裝)

1.新聞英文 2.讀本

805.18　　　　　　　　　　　　　　98004787

© Intermediate Reading 4：新聞宅急通 B

彙　　　編	三民英語編輯小組
發 行 人	劉振強
著作財產權人	三民書局股份有限公司
發 行 所	三民書局股份有限公司
	地址　臺北市復興北路386號
	電話　(02)25006600
	郵撥帳號　0009998–5
門 市 部	(復北店) 臺北市復興北路386號
	(重南店) 臺北市重慶南路一段61號
出版日期	初版一刷　2009年4月
	初版五刷　2018年2月
編　　　號	S 807370

行政院新聞局登記證局版臺業字第○二○○號

有著作權・不准侵害

ISBN　978-957-14-5178-7　（平裝）

http://www.sanmin.com.tw　三民網路書店
※本書如有缺頁、破損或裝訂錯誤，請寄回本公司更換。

序

知識，就是希望；閱讀，就是力量。

在這個資訊爆炸的時代，應該如何選擇真正有用的資訊來吸收？
在考場如戰場的競爭壓力之下，應該如何儲備實力，漂亮地面對挑戰？
身為地球村的一份子，應該如何增進英語實力，與世界接軌？

學習英文的目的，就是要讓自己在這個資訊爆炸的時代之中，突破語言的藩籬，站在吸收新知的制高點之上，以閱讀獲得力量，以知識創造希望！

針對在英文閱讀中可能面對的挑戰，我們費心規劃 Reading Power 系列叢書，希望在學習英語的路上助您一臂之力，讓您輕鬆閱讀、快樂學習。

本系列叢書分為三個等級：
Basic：適用於大考中心公佈之詞彙分級表中第一、二級（前兩千個單字）的範圍；適用於全民英檢初級。
Intermediate：適用於大考中心公佈之詞彙分級表中第三、四級（第兩千到四千個單字）的範圍；適用於全民英檢中級。
Advanced：適用於大考中心公佈之詞彙分級表中第五、六級（第四千到七千個單字）的範圍；適用於全民英檢中高級。
我們希望以這樣的分級方式，讓讀者能針對自己的需求及程度選擇適合的書籍。

誠摯希望在學習英語的路上，這套 Reading Power 系列叢書將伴隨您找到閱讀的力量，發揮知識的光芒！

給讀者的話

　　誠如英語教學大師 H. Douglas Brown 所言:「閱讀」往往與聽、說、寫等語言能力培養有著密不可分的關係。閱讀通常被認為是學習語言的基本能力,這種能力的提升能夠幫助語言學習者更有效地學習 。 至於要如何加強閱讀能力呢?目前最為人所認同的理念包括「真實材料」(authentic material)、「由上而下的閱讀技巧」(top-down strategy) 以及「基模理論」(schema theory) 等。

　　「真實材料」指的是存在於真實情境中的語料,目的是為了使語言學習者能夠接觸到真實情境中使用到的語言,並進行更有意義的學習。本書的取材來自國內外的重要新聞,透過外籍作者的撰寫,設計出適合讀者程度的閱讀內容。「由上而下的閱讀技巧」簡而言之指的就是由整體到部分,這也正是本書的編排理念,從整篇文章的閱讀到文中的單字片語分析,讓讀者可以獲得更全面的了解。最後,「基模理論」是透過現有的想法和知識,納入新的概念,最後內化成自己的知識。讀者倘若對某篇文章內容有基本的認識與了解,必定會提高對這篇文章的興趣;在閱讀過程中,也可以快速掌握重點並理解內容。本書所蒐集的題材皆為近年來熱門話題,藉由讀者本身對該新聞事件的了解,產生共鳴進而提高閱讀效果。

　　在這樣的設計架構下,本書之新聞主題貼近生活,撰文亦力求符合讀者程度,並設計以下單元以增進讀者學習成效:

◆ Reading Comprehension:根據文章內容設計閱讀測驗,涵蓋主旨、細節、類推等出題概念。

◆ Vocabulary:列出文章中關鍵字彙,並提供中文解釋與例句,讓讀者能夠正確使用詞彙。

◆ Idioms & Phrases：列出文章重要片語，並提供中文解釋及例句。

◆ Pop Quiz：針對字彙與片語的小測驗，有選擇、拼字、文意選填等多種題型，提供讀者自我評量的工具。

　　此外，本書後半部附上所有文章之全文翻譯及補充，讓讀者對文章可以有更深入的理解；同時還有精闢的閱讀測驗解析，提供實用的解題技巧。

　　本書之編寫力求完善，但難免有疏漏之處，希望讀者與各界賢達隨時賜教。

三民英語編輯小組　謹誌

Table of Contents

新聞宅急通

翻譯與解析

	略語表
adj.	adjective (形容詞)
adv.	adverb (副詞)
aux.	auxiliary (助動詞)
[C]	countable (可數名詞)
colloq.	colloquial (口語用法)
conj.	conjunction (連接詞)
DO	Direct Object (直接受詞)
fml.	formal (正式用法)
infml.	informal (日常用法)
interj.	interjection (感嘆詞)
IO	Indirect Object (間接受詞)
n.	noun (名詞)
NP	Noun Phrase (名詞片語)
O	Object (受詞)
OC	Object Complement (受詞補語)
pl.	plural (複數)
prep.	preposition (介系詞)
pron.	pronoun (代名詞)
S	Subject (主詞)
SC	Subject Complement (主詞補語)
sing.	singular (單數)
[U]	uncountable (不可數名詞)
usu.	usually (通常地)
V	verb (動詞)
V-ed	past tense (過去式)
Vi	intransitive verb (不及物動詞)
V-ing	present participle (現在分詞)/Gerund (動名詞)
Vpp	past participle (過去分詞)
Vt	transitive verb (及物動詞)

News Messenger

UNIT 01

A New Look at National Stereotypes

December, 2005

We all know that Americans are loud and friendly, the French are romantic, and Japanese people are quiet and polite. But hold on a minute. These common stereotypes, which many people around the world believe, are actually untrue. Recently, a new study has shown that although national stereotypes are widespread, they are usually incorrect.

The results of this study were published in the journal [1]*Science*. In the study, 4,000 people from 49 cultures received surveys instructing them to describe a typical person from their own culture. Then, participants were given another survey and told to describe themselves and people they knew from their culture.

When the two surveys were compared, the results did not match. **In other words**, the ways in which participants thought of a typical person from their own culture and the ways in which they thought of themselves were quite different.

Germans, for example, are often thought to be orderly and efficient. However, as the study shows, most Germans do**n't** believe that they themselves are that way **at all**. They might see themselves as wild, passionate, or even lazy. Though they understand that a stereotype about Germans exists and might even believe that other Germans act this way, they think that they are the exceptions to it.

From the example above, we can see just how unreliable stereotypes are. So, next time you want to use stereotypes to describe someone as a "typical" German or a "stereotypical" person from any country, **think twice**. Perhaps one of the researchers from the study said it best: "National stereotypes can provide some information about a culture, but they do not describe people."

Choose the best answers.

(　　) 1. What is the stereotype of Germans?

    (A) They are very noisy.　　　　(B) They are friendly.

    (C) They do things quickly.　　　(D) They fall in love with people easily.

(　　) 2. Which of the following statements about the research on national stereotypes is true?

    (A) The results of the study show that national stereotypes are usually untrue.

    (B) The participants have to describe a typical person from other cultures.

    (C) The results of the study have not been published yet.

    (D) All of the 4,000 people surveyed are from Asian countries.

(　　) 3. The passage inferred that how participants described themselves and how they thought of a typical person from their own culture were _____ .

    (A) similar　　　(B) matched　　　(C) incorrect　　　(D) different

(　　) 4. The word "**unreliable**" in the last paragraph means "_____."

    (A) uncertain　　　　　　　　(B) unimportant

    (C) undependable　　　　　　(D) understandable

(　　) 5. What does the author think of national stereotypes?

    (A) We shouldn't believe national stereotypes because they are all incorrect.

    (B) National stereotypes let us have some information about a culture.

    (C) People who don't act like their own national stereotypes are just the exceptions.

    (D) We can understand people from different cultures by looking into their national stereotypes.

Vocabulary

1. **stereotype** [ˋstɛrɪəˌtaɪp] *n.* [C] 刻板印象，典型

   stereotypical [ˌstɛrɪəˋtɪpɪk!] *adj.* 刻板化的，老套的

   • It is a stereotype that women should stay at home and cook for her family.

   • I can't find anything new or interesting in that stereotypical love story.

2. **romantic** [rəˋmæntɪk] *adj.* 浪漫的

‧ With music and candlelight, Ben and Jenny are enjoying a romantic dinner.

3. **recently** [ˋrisn̩tlɪ] *adv.* 近來，最近

‧ Jennifer has been busy writing her final report recently.

4. **widespread** [ˋwaɪdˋsprɛd] *adj.* 普及的

‧ MP3 players are widespread now, and you can see people using them everywhere.

5. **publish** [ˋpʌblɪʃ] *vt.* 刊登；出版

‧ Alice was so excited when finding her work published in the newspaper.

‧ The company publishes a fashion magazine that sells very well.

6. **journal** [ˋdʒɝn̩l] *n.* [C] 期刊

‧ *National Geographic* is a journal which is published once a month.

7. **instruct** [ɪnˋstrʌkt] *vt.* 指導，指示

‧ Willy instructed the new worker to operate the machine.

8. **typical** [ˋtɪpɪkl̩] *adj.* 典型的；具代表性的

‧ This modern painting is typical of Alison's work.

9. **participant** [pɚˋtɪsəpənt] *n.* [C] 參加者

‧ After a long discussion, we decided to be the participants of the experiment.

10. **German** [ˋdʒɝmən] *n.* [C] 德國人

‧ Sam is very lazy; he doesn't think he is a typical German at all.

11. **orderly** [ˋɔrdɚlɪ] *adj.* 有條理的

‧ Anne always keeps her room clean and orderly.

12. **efficient** [əˋfɪʃənt] *adj.* 能幹的，有效率的

‧ Ms. Lee is an efficient secretary and trusted by her boss.

13. **passionate** [ˋpæʃənɪt] *adj.* 熱情的

‧ Elaine gave her boyfriend a passionate kiss on his birthday.

14. **exception** [ɪkˋsɛpʃən] *n.* [C] 例外

‧ Mr. Wang treats his students equally; he won't make an exception.

15. **unreliable** [ˌʌnrɪˋlaɪəbl̩] *adj.* 不可靠的

‧ Don't believe what Frank says to you; he is unreliable.

16. **researcher** [rɪˋsɝtʃɚ] *n.* [C] 研究人員

‧ Researchers do lots of experiments in order to find a new medicine to cure the disease.

17. **information** [ˌɪnfɚˋmeʃən] *n.* [U] 資訊

‧ We can get a lot of information about almost any subject on the Internet.

Idioms & Phrases

1. **in other words**　換句話說
   ・I am very busy today. In other words, I can't have lunch with you.

2. **not...at all**　一點也不
   ・Who told you I liked that movie? In fact, I don't like it at all.

3. **think twice**　重新考慮，三思
   ・You had better think twice before meeting your online friend alone.

Pop Quiz

Choose the best answer to each of the following sentences.

(　　) 1. Every student should go to school before 7:30 a.m. and you can make no
_____ .
  (A) action　　　(B) publication　　(C) passion　　(D) exception

(　　) 2. There is _____ concern about the environmental problems, such as global
warming and pollution.
  (A) unreliable　(B) widespread　(C) efficient　　(D) terrific

(　　) 3. Daniel's dad _____ him how to drive when he was eighteen.
  (A) published　(B) included　　(C) instructed　(D) excused

(　　) 4. The _____ are making a careful study of the new medicine to learn more
about its influence on the human body.
  (A) stereotypes　(B) records　　(C) researchers　(D) messages

(　　) 5. The boy couldn't find his way home; _____ , he got lost.
  (A) in other words　(B) think twice　(C) for example　(D) as if

UNIT 02

Another Problem for [1]China Airlines

September, 2007

On August 20, 2007, China Airlines Flight 120 ended badly — and dramatically — with a frightening explosion in Japan. The plane, a [2]Boeing 737-800, had departed from Taipei that day and landed at Naha Airport in [3]Okinawa. As the plane came to a stop on the runway, however, one of its engines began to smoke and burn.

An alert ground crew member at the airport noticed the problem and notified the plane's captain. The plane's crew then immediately began to make preparations for evacuating everyone **on board** the plane. **Thanks to** their quick action, all 157 passengers were able to exit the plane in just a few minutes, and dramatic video footage showed passengers sliding down the plane's emergency slides. Moments later, the China Airlines plane burst into a giant fireball of flames. Fortunately, all of the passengers and crew members were able to make it to safety, with only a few minor injuries, and no one was killed or seriously hurt in the incident.

The explosion in Japan came as a blow to China Airlines' efforts to improve its reputation and safety record, which [4]CNN once called "one of the worst safety records of any airline in the world." Before this incident, experts had believed that China Airlines had **turned the corner** and started to make lasting improvements, since the company's last major accident had occurred five years earlier. This latest explosion, however, has once again raised concerns — and fears — about the airline.

Investigators have already **ruled out** terrorism as a possible cause of the explosion. Instead, they said that a loose bolt most likely punctured a fuel tank in the plane's right wing, causing a fuel leak. Investigations into the cause of the explosion and into the way China Airlines maintains its planes continue at this time.

Choose the best answers.

(   ) 1. The airplane which exploded on August 20 _____ .

    (A) is a Boeing 747   (B) is China Airlines Flight 800

    (C) departed from Okinawa   (D) carried 157 passengers

(   ) 2. The explosion of the China Airlines airplane happened _____ .

    (A) in the sky before landing in Japan

    (B) after all the passengers exited the plane

    (C) in the air right after departing from Taiwan

    (D) before taking off from the airport in Taiwan

(   ) 3. What does "**turn the corner**" mean in the third paragraph?

    (A) To change a direction and go somewhere else.

    (B) To get over a difficult situation and start to improve.

    (C) To fly around in circles and make a perfect landing.

    (D) To break the world record by making several turns in the sky.

(   ) 4. Which of the following statements is true?

    (A) According to some experts, the explosion of the airplane might be caused by a loose bolt.

    (B) China Airlines' last accident occurred three years ago.

    (C) CNN praised China Airlines for handling the explosion accident well.

    (D) Some investigators suspected that terrorism was involved in this accident.

(   ) 5. What is the main idea of this passage?

    (A) China Airlines has set a good example of crisis management in this accident.

    (B) China Airlines made a dramatic landing in Japan and proved that its pilots had good flying skills.

    (C) The explosion at Naha Airport has once again raised concerns about China Airlines.

    (D) It is important to follow the instructions given by flight attendants in case of emergency.

Vocabulary

1. **dramatically** [drə`mætɪklɪ] *adv.* 戲劇性地，引人注目地

   dramatic [drə`mætɪk] *adj.* 戲劇般的，引人注目的

   · Because of Chien-Ming Wang's success in MLB, the number of the Yankees fans has increased dramatically in Taiwan.

   · Since the late 1990s, the Internet has brought dramatic changes to our world.

2. **explosion** [ɪk`sploʒən] *n.* [C] 爆炸

   · The gas explosion broke all the windows of the house and caused a big fire.

3. **depart** [dɪ`pɑrt] *vi.* 出發

   · About three hundred passengers were departing for Nagoya on that flight.

4. **alert** [ə`lɝt] *adj.* 警覺的，留神的

   · The hunter was alert to every sound and movement in the forest.

5. **crew** [kru] *n.* [C] 機組人員；工作人員

   · Three hundred people, including the crew, were killed in the plane crash.

6. **notify** [`notə‚faɪ] *vt.* 告知，通知

   · Please notify me of any suspicious activity that may be going on in this area.

7. **evacuate** [ɪ`vækju‚et] *vt.* 疏散，撤離

   · People in the village had been evacuated before the typhoon approached.

8. **footage** [`futɪdʒ] *n.* [U] 一段影片

   · The old film footage was shot in France during World War I.

9. **emergency** [ɪ`mɝdʒənsɪ] *n.* [U][C] 緊急情況

   · Call 119 in case of emergency.

10. **flame** [flem] *n.* [C] 火焰

    · In just a few minutes, the wooden house burned down in flames.

11. **minor** [`maɪnɚ] *adj.* 不嚴重的

    · Thank God! Frank only received minor burns in the fire.

12. **injury** [`ɪndʒərɪ] *n.* [C] 傷害

    · The little girl suffered serious head injuries in the car accident.

13. **reputation** [‚rɛpjə`teʃən] *n.* [C] 名聲，聲望

    · The successful operation has earned Dr. Chen a good reputation as one of the world's best surgeons.

14. **terrorism** [ˋtɛrə͵rɪzəm] *n.* [U] 恐怖主義，恐怖行動

· The United States is one of the main targets of Islamist terrorism.

15. **bolt** [bolt] *n.* [C] 螺栓

· You have to fasten the bolt tightly, or the window might fall down.

16. **puncture** [ˋpʌŋktʃɚ] *vt.* 刺破

· A nail punctured the rear tire, making my car unable to run.

17. **fuel** [ˋfjuəl] *n.* [U] 燃料

· Using coal as fuel to produce electricity will cause serious air pollution.

18. **leak** [lik] *n.* [C] 漏出，漏洞

· Even a small gas leak may cause a huge fire or a terrible explosion.

Idioms & Phrases

1. **on board**　在機上／船上／車上 (的)

· The bus driver started the engine after all the passengers got on board.

2. **thanks to**　幸虧，由於

· Thanks to your advice, I was able to get the job done in time.

3. **turn the corner**　好轉，度過難關

· The patient was once very ill, but he has turned the corner now.

4. **rule out**　排除

· The police have ruled out the possibility that the woman committed suicide.

Pop Quiz

Fill in each blank with the correct answer to complete the sentence.

(A) emergency	(B) terrorism	(C) departed	(D) dramatically
(E) evacuated	(F) turned the corner	(G) thanks to	(H) on board

1. It is said that a couple's life changes _____ when they have a baby.

2. The experiment was a big success, _____ everybody's efforts.

3. The plane made an _____ landing in the violent storm.

4. The police _____ all the people in the building shortly before the explosion.

5. There were totally 250 passengers _____ the plane.

UNIT 03

Attention and Assistance Needed in Asia

This May, two Asian countries were struck by separate natural disasters. The first occurred in Myanmar, also known as [1]Burma. At the beginning of May, a powerful tropical cyclone slammed into this country. The cyclone, called [2]Nargis, caused severe devastation, killing thousands and leaving thousands more homeless and without power or clean water. Initially, Myanmar's secretive military government was reluctant to give out details about the destruction there and refused offers of international assistance. However, as the extent of the damage became clear, the government relented and slowly began to accept emergency supplies from other countries.

Then, on May 12 at 2:28 p.m., China was rocked by a powerful earthquake. The quake, which measured 7.9 on the [3]Richter scale, was the biggest to hit China in more than thirty years. Sichuan Province, in the west of China, was most affected by this natural disaster. The earthquake's epicenter was in Wenchuan County, which is about 80 kilometers northwest of Chengdu, the capital of Sichuan. In northern Sichuan, thousands were killed as buildings collapsed throughout the area.

News of the earthquake grabbed headlines in Taiwan and dominated the news around the world in the days that followed. Many news reports focused on the 6,898 classrooms that were destroyed in the earthquake. **In total**, 65,000 people died in the earthquake, and 360,000 were injured. More than 23,000 people are still missing.

Although the Sichuan earthquake has received extensive media coverage and worldwide attention, the destruction in Myanmar was just as extensive. Reports say that 78,000 people died in the cyclone and 56,000 are still missing. One million people are now also homeless because of the cyclone. **In addition**, experts fear that many more will die in Myanmar, because of delayed relief aid and food shortages.

In times of trouble, people need help. Sadly, the government in Myanmar has been slow to accept offers of assistance from other countries. In addition, the international news media have focused on the disaster in China, instead of on the disaster in Myanmar. **As a result**, many people don't know how grave the situation is in Myanmar. One thing is clear: the victims of the recent natural disasters in both Myanmar and China need the world's attention and assistance now more than ever.

Reading Comprehension

Choose the best answers.

(   ) 1. About the statistics for the two disasters, which of the following is NOT true?

      (A) 65,000 died in the earthquake.

      (B) 56,000 are still missing in the cyclone.

      (C) More people died in the earthquake than in the cyclone.

      (D) More people are missing in the cyclone than in the earthquake.

(   ) 2. Which of the following statements is true?

      (A) A serious earthquake struck Burma in May.

      (B) A tropical cyclone slammed into Wenchuan County on May 12.

      (C) The most serious earthquake in China over thirty years happened in Sichuan.

      (D) Myanmar's military government killed thousands of its people.

(   ) 3. Wenchuan County is _____ .

      (A) the capital of Sichuan

      (B) where the earthquake's epicenter is located

      (C) a few miles southeast of Chengdu

      (D) the biggest city in Sichuan Province

(   ) 4. What has been the international news reports' focus after the two disasters?

      (A) The Sichuan earthquake.

      (B) The 6,898 classrooms destroyed in the cyclone.

      (C) The cyclone in Myanmar.

      (D) The international assistance.

(   ) 5. What does the word "**grave**" mean in the last paragraph?

      (A) Serious.   (B) Thankful.   (C) Easy.   (D) Angry.

Vocabulary

1. **assistance** [əˋsɪstəns] *n.* [U] 幫助，協助
   · Can I be of any assistance? You look worried.

2. **disaster** [dɪˋzæstɚ] *n.* [C] 災難
   · The 921 earthquake in 1999 is one of the most serious disasters in Taiwan.

3. **tropical** [ˋtrɑpɪkl̩] *adj.* 熱帶的
   · It's sad to learn that the tropical rain forest is being destroyed at a fast rate.

4. **cyclone** [ˋsaɪklon] *n.* [C] 氣旋
   · A cyclone is a strong and fast-moving storm.

5. **severe** [səˋvɪr] *adj.* 嚴重的
   · Mr. Brown suffered severe injuries in the car accident. He lost one of his legs.

6. **devastation** [͵dɛvəsˋteʃən] *n.* [U] 毀壞
   · The war caused complete devastation in the country.

7. **initially** [ɪˋnɪʃəlɪ] *adv.* 最初地，一開始地
   · The baseball game, initially planned for today, was canceled due to the weather.

8. **reluctant** [rɪˋlʌktənt] *adj.* 勉為其難的，不情願的
   · The beach party was so much fun that we were reluctant to leave.

9. **extent** [ɪkˋstɛnt] *n.* [U] 程度，範圍
   · The extent of the damage caused by the earthquake is still unknown.

10. **relent** [rɪˋlɛnt] *vi.* 變溫和，緩和
    · My parents' attitude relented after I apologized to them.

11. **province** [ˋprɑvɪns] *n.* [C] 省，州
    · Ontario is the second largest province in Canada.

12. **epicenter** [ˋɛpɪ͵sɛntɚ] *n.* [C] 震央
    · The epicenter of the 921 earthquake is in Chichi, Nantou.

13. **collapse** [kəˋlæps] *vi.* 倒塌，坍塌
    · Lots of houses collapsed when the earthquake struck.

14. **headline** [ˋhɛd͵laɪn] *n.* [C] (報紙等的) 標題
    · The president's scandal has made the headlines for many weeks.

15. **dominate** [ˋdɑmə͵net] *vt.* 主導，控制
    · Although money is important, it should not dominate our lives.

16. **extensive** [ɪkˋstɛnsɪv] *adj.* 廣泛的
   · I did extensive reading in the free time to improve my reading ability.
17. **coverage** [ˋkʌvərɪdʒ] *n.* [U] 新聞報導內容
   · China's violent suppression of Tibet has attracted international press coverage.
18. **relief** [rɪˋlif] *n.* [U] 救濟物資
   · A charity concert was held soon after the earthquake to raise disaster relief fund.
19. **grave** [grev] *adj.* 嚴重的，重大的
   · Don't go back to the burning house! You could put yourself in grave danger.
20. **victim** [ˋvɪktɪm] *n.* [C] 受害者
   · The victims of the car accident were rushed to the hospital immediately.

Idioms & Phrases

1. **in total**　總計，合計
   · The team won six games, and lost three. So, they played nine games in total.
2. **in addition**　此外
   · We love our country. In addition, we respect our national flag.
3. **as a result**　因此
   · Jim kept smoking against his doctor's advice. As a result, he became very ill.

Pop Quiz

Fill in each blank with the correct word or phrase to complete the passage. Make changes if necessary.

as a result	cyclone	devastation	victim	in addition	disaster

　　Animals seem to have the ability to know about natural [1]_____ such as earthquakes or [2]_____ before they happen. Once, in a Chinese village, the people saw the animals around them behaving strangely. The dogs barked all the time and the mice ran out of their holes. [3]_____, the village was struck by an earthquake that caused [4]_____ the following day. [5]_____, when dangers come from the sea, animals and birds leave the sea shore and travel far away. So if we pay more attention to the animals around us, we can save ourselves and won't become the [6]_____ of natural disasters.

UNIT 04

Bad Behavior and Celebrity Mistakes

January, 2007

Over the past few months, some celebrities in both Taiwan and the United States have been grabbing headlines for their bad behavior. In Taiwan, seven entertainers have tested positive for illegal drug use. In the United States, [1]Miss USA was criticized for underage drinking.

In Taiwan, police officers discovered in a luxurious apartment in Taipei hundreds of marijuana plants and a cell phone with the phone numbers of several well-known entertainers. Investigators then decided to **call in** these stars for questioning. At first, all of the stars denied that they had used drugs. Two stars, the TV show hosts Tuo Tsung-Kang and Chu Chung-Heng, even held a press conference to deny they had ever smoked marijuana. However, the next day, Tuo and Chu both tearfully admitted that they had indeed used illegal drugs.

A few weeks later, hair and urine samples proved that seven of the stars had actually used illegal drugs, including marijuana and cocaine. Although most of the stars claimed that they had only used these drugs in other Asian countries, all of them will have to **go through** mandatory [2]drug rehabilitation programs.

Another tearful press conference was held in the United States. Miss USA [3]Tara Conner admitted to underage drinking at nightclubs in New York City. However, after the beauty queen met with [4]Donald Trump, the famous billionaire who owns the [5]Miss Universe Organization, Trump decided to give Conner a second chance. At their press conference, Trump said that Conner was a "good person" with a "good heart" who had made some mistakes. She will be allowed to retain her Miss USA title, but she must enter a rehabilitation program and undergo drug testing.

Many believe that these incidents should **serve as** a lesson to stars and public figures. When a star makes a mistake, he or she can choose to either admit or deny it. However, stars should know that if they decide to lie, then the general public and their fans will make their own judgments after the truth has been revealed. In addition, since young people often imitate what famous people do, celebrities today must be more careful about the way they act and brave enough to face the consequences of their mistakes.

Choose the best answers.

(   ) 1. Why did Tuo and Chu hold a press conference in the first place?

    (A) They wanted to announce that they discovered marijuana in an apartment.

    (B) They wanted to announce that they were under the police's investigation.

    (C) They wanted to announce that they had never smoked marijuana before.

    (D) They wanted to announce that they would have a new TV show.

(   ) 2. The police officers called in some stars for questioning because _____ .

    (A) they found marijuana plants and a cell phone with the stars' phone numbers

    (B) they were told these stars had used drugs in other Asian countries

    (C) they got the hair and urine samples from the stars

    (D) they watched the press conferences held by the stars

(   ) 3. After the press conference, Miss USA Tara Conner would NOT _____ .

    (A) undergo drug testing

    (B) retain her Miss USA title

    (C) be allowed to make the same mistake

    (D) enter a rehabilitation program

(   ) 4. Which of the following statements is NOT true?

    (A) Young people would imitate what famous people do.

    (B) Fans would never think their idols are wrong.

    (C) Stars should be more careful about their own behavior.

    (D) Stars should be brave enough to admit their own mistakes.

(   ) 5. The phrase "**serve as**" in the last paragraph can be replaced by "_____ ."

    (A) be   (B) save   (C) copy   (D) permit

Vocabulary

1. **entertainer** [ˌɛntɚˋtenɚ] *n.* [C] 藝人
   · As an entertainer, Kathy is busy in attending different TV shows.

2. **illegal** [ɪˋligl̩] *adj.* 非法的
   · Drunk driving is illegal in almost every country.

3. **criticize** [ˋkrɪtəˌsaɪz] *vt.* 批評
   · Harold is difficult to get along with because he likes to criticize others.

4. **luxurious** [lʌgˋʒʊrɪəs] *adj.* 豪華的，奢侈的
   · The luxurious hotel room will cost you NT$15,000 one night.

5. **marijuana** [ˌmɑrɪˋhwɑnə] *n.* [U] 大麻
   · It is illegal to plant marijuana in your own garden in this country.

6. **press conference** [ˋprɛs ˋkɑnfərəns] *n.* [C] 記者會
   · The singer held a press conference to talk about her new album.

7. **urine** [ˋjʊrɪn] *n.* [U] 尿液
   · The old man was worried because he found there was blood in his urine.

8. **sample** [ˋsæmpl̩] *n.* [C] 採樣，樣本
   · The salesperson went from door to door to give the samples of his product.

9. **actually** [ˋæktʃʊəlɪ] *adv.* 實際上
   · Willy looks young, but he is actually forty years old.

10. **cocaine** [koˋken] *n.* [U] 古柯鹼
    · Sam was caught using cocaine and was sent to the police.

11. **mandatory** [ˋmændəˌtorɪ] *adj.* 強制的
    · According to the law, wearing a helmet is mandatory for anyone who rides a motorcycle.

12. **billionaire** [ˌbɪljənˋɛr] *n.* [C] 億萬富翁
    · J.K. Rowling became a billionaire by creating *Harry Potter*, a series of seven fantasy novels.

13. **retain** [rɪˋten] *vt.* 保留
    · My mom let me retain the comic books, so I didn't have to throw them away.

14. **undergo** [ˌʌndɚˋgo] *vt.* 接受 (治療、檢查等) (～, underwent, undergone)
    · Before serving in the army, the man had to undergo a physical examination.

15. **incident** [`ɪnsədn̩t] *n.* [C] 事件

· The 921 earthquake was surely the most serious incident in Taiwan in 1999.

16. **figure** [`fɪgjɚ] *n.* [C] 人物

· Abraham Lincoln is one of the important figures in American history.

17. **imitate** [`ɪmə,tet] *vt.* 模仿

· It is hard to imitate how Vicky talks because she has such a unique voice.

18. **consequence** [`kɑnsə,kwɛns] *n.* [C] 後果

· After making the decision, you have to face the consequences of it on your own.

Idioms & Phrases

1. **call in**　請來

· To find out the murderer, the police called in some witnesses to get more clues.

2. **go through**　經歷

· The man went through many difficulties before he reached success.

3. **serve as**　當成…

· My sofa can serve as a bed, so if you like, you can stay in my house tonight.

Pop Quiz

Choose the answer that is closest in meaning with the underlined part.

(　　) 1. Children like to imitate their parents' behavior.

(A) undergo　　　(B) imagine　　　(C) copy　　　(D) deny

(　　) 2. Jeff retains his sense of humor even in difficulties.

(A) criticizes　　(B) notifies　　　(C) reduces　　　(D) keeps

(　　) 3. Sally said she went to the library, but she actually went to the theater.

(A) dramatically　(B) really　　　(C) tearfully　　　(D) initially

(　　) 4. Martin Luther King, Jr. is an important figure in the African-American civil rights movement.

(A) incident　　　(B) person　　　(C) judge　　　(D) victim

(　　) 5. The man has gone through many wars; he looks much older for his age.

(A) experienced　(B) revealed　　(C) added　　　(D) punctured

UNIT 05

Bad Start for 2008 [1]Olympics

May, 2008

The Olympics **is supposed to** be a time of peace and goodwill, and one of the highlights has traditionally been the journey of the Olympic torch from [2]Greece to the country hosting the event. This year, however, this journey has been disrupted by demonstrations, protests, and even fights.

The problems began before the Olympic torch was even lit. In the early part of 2008, [3]Tibetan monks and nuns, **along with** ordinary Tibetans, began to protest for greater freedom in parts of Tibet. A few protestors even **called for** Tibetan independence and an end to Chinese rule there. In the weeks that followed, several people, both Tibetans and Chinese people, were killed in the unrest. Though the protests were not successful in ending the Chinese occupation of Tibet, they were able to draw world attention to the situation there.

As a result, when the Olympic flame traveled to several different European countries on its journey to [4]Beijing, it was met **not only** by Olympic supporters **but also** by protestors **as well**. Particularly in England and France, the Olympic-torch relay was interrupted on several occasions by demonstrators, most of whom were Tibetan-freedom activists. On some occasions, the protestors interrupted the event by simply holding up Tibetan flags. On other occasions, though, they actually attempted to grab the Olympic torch and extinguish the flame.

With less than a hundred days left to the opening ceremonies in Beijing, the Olympic torch is now in China, and it is safe to say that it will most likely be welcomed by cheering crowds there rather than by protestors. However, it is still causing controversy, as Chinese officials said that they would continue with their plan to carry the flame to the top of [5]Mount Everest, despite criticism of this move as uncaring and risky.

It remains unclear whether there will be further protests at the Olympics in August. One thing is sure, though: the road to the 2008 Olympics in Beijing has been a rocky one **so far**.

Choose the best answers.

(　　) 1. What has been the traditional highlight of the Olympics?

  (A) The journey of the Olympic torch.　(B) The demonstrations in Europe.

  (C) The protests of Tibetans.　 (D) The fights of monks and nuns.

(　　) 2. What caused the mess during the journey of the Olympic torch?

  (A) The claim that China will send the torch to Mount Everest.

  (B) The protests for greater freedom in parts of Tibet.

  (C) The fact that the torch will not go through England and France.

  (D) The event that the Tibetan-freedom activists burned the Tibetan flags.

(　　) 3. What does the author mean in the last paragraph?

  (A) There will be more protests at the Olympics in August.

  (B) The road to the top of Mount Everest is rocky.

  (C) The road to Beijing is very rocky.

  (D) We don't know if the Olympics in Beijing will go successfully.

(　　) 4. What movement did China plan to do that was accused of being uncaring and risky?

  (A) They are planning to carry the Olympic flame to the top of Mount Everest.

  (B) They are going to occupy Tibet.

  (C) They are going to extinguish the Olympic flame.

  (D) They are going to hold up the Tibetan flags in the opening ceremonies of the Olympics.

(　　) 5. Which of the following words is the closest in meaning with the word "**disrupt**" in the first paragraph?

  (A) Encounter.　 (B) Celebrate.　 (C) Interrupt.　 (D) Support.

Vocabulary

1. **goodwill** [`gʊd`wɪl] *n.* [U] 善意，友好

 · I invited the new student to join our reading club as a gesture of goodwill.

2. **highlight** [`haɪ,laɪt] *n.* [C] (活動中) 最精采的部分

 · The Great Wall of China was the highlight of our trip.

3. **journey** [ˋdʒɝnɪ] *n.* [C] 旅程
   · Jerry wrote a book describing his journey through Japan.

4. **torch** [tɔrtʃ] *n.* [C] 火炬
   · The Olympic torch is now carried by a famous runner.

5. **disrupt** [dɪsˋrʌpt] *vt.* 使混亂，使中斷
   · The students disrupted the class by keeping talking to each other in class.

6. **demonstration** [ˌdɛmənˋstreʃən] *n.* [C] 示威
   · There was a demonstration against the government's new tax law.

7. **protest** [ˋprotɛst] *n.* [C] 抗議
   · Parents throughout the country made a protest against the violent TV show.

8. **monk** [mʌŋk] *n.* [C] 僧侶，和尚
   · Dave left his life of luxury and became a monk leading a simple life.

9. **nun** [nʌn] *n.* [C] 修女，尼姑
   · Tzu Chi was founded in 1966 by a nun, Cheng Yen.

10. **occupation** [ˌɑkjəˋpeʃən] *n.* [U] 佔領
    · The German occupation of France lasted for four years during World War II.

11. **relay** [rɪˋle] *n.* [C] 接力
    · The teacher asked us to stand up and read the article in relays.

12. **interrupt** [ˌɪntəˋrʌpt] *vt.* 打斷，中斷
    · Ian was interrupted by a call when watching a basketball game on TV.

13. **occasion** [əˋkeʒən] *n.* [C] 場合，機會
    · My sister only wears skirts on special occasions.

14. **activist** [ˋæktɪvɪst] *n.* [C] 行動主義者；激進份子
    · Mr. Li is an animal right activist. He always tries his best to protect animals.

15. **attempt** [əˋtɛmpt] *vt.* 試圖
    · Jack once attempted to stop smoking, but he failed.

16. **extinguish** [ɪkˋstɪŋgwɪʃ] *vt.* 撲滅 (火等)
    · The firefighters tried hard to extinguish the fire but in vain.

17. **ceremony** [ˋsɛrəˌmonɪ] *n.* [C] 儀式，典禮
    · Kevin thought it an honor to give a speech at the graduation ceremony.

18. **controversy** [ˋkɑntrəˌvɝsɪ] *n.* [U] 爭論
    · Mr. Gore's campaign speech caused a great deal of controversy.

19. **criticism** [`krɪtəˌsɪzəm] *n.* [U] 批評

· Ken is self-centered and seldom cares about others' criticism.

Idioms & Phrases

1. **be supposed to**   應該

· You are not supposed to smoke in the non-smoking area.

2. **along with**   與…一起

· Learning a language along with its culture will help you master that language.

3. **call for**   呼籲，要求

· The teacher called for his students' help to do the experiment.

4. **not only...but (also)...**   不僅…而且…

· We not only went to the zoo but also had a delicious dinner last weekend.

5. **as well**   也

· The singer's new album brought her a lot of money and fame as well.

6. **so far**   到目前為止

· I've not finished the job so far, and I'll let you know when I do.

Pop Quiz

Choose the best answer to each of the following sentences.

(   ) 1. Mr. Wu took part in a _____ against building a new chemical plant in his hometown.

(A) situation   (B) demonstration (C) occupation   (D) controversy

(   ) 2. Please make sure to _____ your cigarette before you leave.

(A) disrupt   (B) recognize   (C) extinguish   (D) injure

(   ) 3. The _____ of the festival was the fireworks display at midnight.

(A) goodwill   (B) torch   (C) highlight   (D) occasion

(   ) 4. Ben _____ arrive at the meeting at 9 a.m., but now he is late.

(A) was supposed to   (B) was about to

(C) called for   (D) fought for

(   ) 5. Adam is a successful businessperson and a famous writer _____.

(A) along with   (B) rather than   (C) in addition   (D) as well

UNIT 06

Card Slaves: A New Problem in Taiwan

April, 2006

Taiwan is facing one of its biggest problems in years. It is not [1]bird flu or the return of [2]SARS—it is credit-card debts.

The problem began a few years ago when banks started to offer promotions of credit cards, and it became easy for people to get a credit card. For example, some banks offered a variety of free gifts to attract people's attention. Other banks offered credit cards with no annual fee. Eventually, competition between banks to get more customers became so fierce that some banks started to offer credit cards to students and people without steady jobs. Credit-card representatives even **set up** application tables in shopping malls and supermarkets, so that it would be more convenient for people to apply for a card. Meanwhile, applying online became another easy way to get a credit card.

As a result, 9 million people in Taiwan now have **at least** one credit card, and most of these people have, **on average**, four to five cards. 2.6 million credit-card holders in Taiwan also have outstanding credit-card debts. These people, often called "card slaves," owe large amounts of money, and each person has an average debt of NT$330,000. Sadly, some "card slaves" give up hope. Police officials said that over the past few months, about 40 people a month had committed suicide because of credit-card problems.

To solve the problem of credit-card debts in Taiwan, experts said that banks should stop making it so easy for people to get credit cards. They also said that the general public in Taiwan should be taught how to use credit cards properly. Moreover, some said that the government officials should make changes to the [3]Banking Law, so that applying for a credit card will be a stricter and more regulated process.

Reading Comprehension

Choose the best answers.

(　　) 1. "**A card slave**" refers to _____ .

    (A) a person who promotes credit cards

    (B) a person who has too many credit cards

    (C) a person with huge credit-card debts

    (D) a cardholder without a steady job

(　　) 2. Which of the following statements about cardholders in Taiwan is NOT true?

    (A) Some of the cardholders are students or people without regular salary.

    (B) 9 million cardholders have, on average, four to five cards.

    (C) About 40 card slaves a month have killed themselves over the past few months.

    (D) 2.6 million cardholders have outstanding credit-card debts.

(　　) 3. Which of the following statements about card-slave problems is NOT true?

    (A) The card-slave problems should be brought under control by not only the government but also the banks.

    (B) The banks should ask the debt-collecting companies to collect debts from card slaves.

    (C) The credit-card debts have caused new problems for the government.

    (D) The banks should take action and make the process of applying for a credit card stricter.

(　　) 4. The word "**fierce**" in the second paragraph means "_____ ."

    (A) efficient   (B) controversial

    (C) intense   (D) affective

(　　) 5. We can infer from the passage that _____ .

    (A) the credit-card debts have recently been one of the causes of suicide

    (B) the banks should bear the whole responsibility for card-slave problems

    (C) bad credit-card debts are estimated to be a total of 2.6 billion NT dollars

    (D) half cardholders in Taiwan have trouble paying off their credit-card debts

Vocabulary

1. **slave** [slev] *n.* [C] 奴隸
   · Kelly was forced by her stepmother to do everything in the house like a slave.

2. **promotion** [prə`moʃən] *n.* [C] 促銷活動
   · The bookstore was having a sales promotion and attracted many customers.

3. **variety** [və`raɪətɪ] *n.* [U] 各式各樣，種種
   · This restaurant offers a variety of Thai food.

4. **annual** [`ænjʊəl] *adj.* 全年的；一年一次的
   · The annual rainfall in Kaohsiung this year is 1,134 mm.
   · The annual music festival in Kenting is usually held in spring.

5. **eventually** [ɪ`vɛntʃʊəlɪ] *adv.* 終於，最後
   · After years' hard work, Joe eventually realized his dream of being a doctor.

6. **competition** [ˌkɑmpə`tɪʃən] *n.* [U] 競爭，角逐
   · There is keen competition to enter that famous university.

7. **fierce** [fɪrs] *adj.* 激烈的
   · The competition between the two soccer teams was fierce. It was a close game.

8. **steady** [`stɛdɪ] *adj.* 固定的
   · Jacky is dating with many girls. He does not have a steady girlfriend.

9. **representative** [ˌrɛprɪ`zɛntətɪv] *n.* [C] 代表，代理人
   · Henry will be the representative of our company at the meeting.

10. **application** [ˌæplə`keʃən] *n.* [U] 申請；[C] 申請書
    apply [ə`plaɪ] *vi.* 申請
    · Mary was sad because her application to the college was turned down.
    · Please fill in the application and send it back by the end of this month.
    · Kevin is going to apply for a job in that computer company.

11. **meanwhile** [`min͵hwaɪl] *adv.* 同時
    · My brother was playing basketball and I was swimming meanwhile.

12. **outstanding** [`aʊt`stændɪŋ] *adj.* 未付款的；傑出的
    · I still have some outstanding debts and I will pay them off by next month.
    · A-mei is one of the most outstanding singers in Taiwan.

13. **owe** [o] *vt.* 欠 (債…等)

· I still owe Jimmy one thousand NT dollars and I will pay him back next week.

14. **commit** [kə`mɪt] *vt.* 犯 (罪等) (~, committed, committed)

　· The criminal who committed several crimes was sent to jail eventually.

15. **suicide** [`suə,saɪd] *n.* [U] 自殺

　· Committing suicide is never a good way to solve problems.

16. **moreover** [mor`ovɚ] *adv.* 此外，再者

　· This dress looks great on you. Moreover, it's not expensive at all.

17. **regulate** [`rɛgjə,let] *vt.* 規定，管理

　· The boss made new rules to regulate his workers.

18. **process** [`prɑsɛs] *n.* [C] 程序，程序

　· Salt is produced by an entirely new process now.

Idioms & Phrases

1. **set up**　設立

　· This factory was set up by Tom's father in 1983.

2. **at least**　至少

　· It will take me at least ten minutes to walk from here to the MRT station.

3. **on average**　平均

　· Most students in Taiwan spend, on average, two hours a day watching TV.

Pop Quiz

Fill in each blank with the correct word or phrase to complete the sentence. Make changes if necessary.

meanwhile	commit	moreover	variety	regulate
owe	fierce	steady	at least	set up

1. People can eat a _____ of snacks in the Shilin Night Market.
2. There used to be _____ competition in weapons between the United States and Russia.
3. The bus is huge and can take, _____, fifty people.
4. Yesterday, the police caught a man who had _____ a serious crime.
5. Maggie is cooking dinner; _____, her husband is setting the table.

UNIT 07

"Code" Opens with Big Box Office and Controversy

June, 2006

The Da Vinci Code, a controversial new movie, is now in theaters around the world. It is definitely a hit, since it has earned more than US$230 million so far.

Based on the best-selling novel of the same name, the movie was directed by [1]Ron Howard, and it stars Tom Hanks. It tells the story of a Harvard professor named Robert Langdon, who is asked to help the French police investigate a murder at the [2]Louvre Museum in Paris. During the investigation, Langdon discovers different symbols, codes, and clues that lead him to uncover the shocking relationship between a secret society and the Christian religion.

Though it was popular at the box office, The Da Vinci Code disappointed many film critics. Some said that it was only an average film, and some called it boring. Other critics even said that the two-and-a-half-hour movie was too long, because the actors in the film, including Tom Hanks, did not give exciting performances.

In addition, a few religious groups also criticized the movie. They said that its story was disrespectful to Christians, since the film claims that Jesus Christ was married and had children. The movie also implies that the Catholic Church has tried to **cover up** the "truth" about Jesus for years. As a result, the [3]Vatican denounced the movie. Angry Christians in Greece also called for the movie to be banned, and some Christians in India even went on a hunger strike to protest the film.

Despite considerable criticism by some conservative Christians and many movie critics, people around the world continue to flock to theaters to see The Da Vinci Code. Some love the novel and are interested in seeing the film version of the story, while others are fans of Tom Hanks and want to see his latest movie. Still many people just want to **see for themselves** what the controversy over The Da Vinci Code is all about.

Choose the best answers.

(   ) 1. *The Da Vinci Code* has earned _____ so far.

    (A) more than NT$ 230 million dollars (B) more than US$ 230 million dollars

    (C) less than NT$ 230 million dollars   (D) less than US$ 230 million dollars

(   ) 2. Some film critics think that *The Da Vinci Code* _____ .

    (A) is an exciting and excellent movie of 2006

    (B) avoids all the controversial parts from the novel

    (C) reveals the mystery between Jesus and Christianity

    (D) is too long because the actors in the film do not perform well

(   ) 3. What does the word "**flock**" mean in the last paragraph?

    (A) A group of people go to the church.

    (B) A group of people say the same thing.

    (C) A group of people gather to do something.

    (D) A group of people fight against something.

(   ) 4. Which of the following statements about *The Da Vinci Code* is true?

    (A) It is not so successful as its original novel.

    (B) It starts from the murder at the Louvre Museum, Paris.

    (C) It is a big box office movie based on a historical event.

    (D) It is a story about how Leonardo da Vinci breaks the code in his own painting.

(   ) 5. According to the fourth paragraph, we could find that _____ .

    (A) the Vatican decided not to ban the movie

    (B) many Muslims protested against the movie

    (C) many religious groups supported this movie

    (D) the description of Jesus' marriage and his children is the controversy of the movie

Vocabulary

1. **code** [kod] *n.* [C] 密碼

    · This is a letter written in codes, so I can't understand it.

2. **box office** [`bɑks ˌɔfɪs] *n.* [C] 票房

   · The movie has taken more than US$50 million at the box office during one week.

3. **definitely** [`dɛfənɪtlɪ] *adv.* 無疑地

   · Shakespeare is definitely the most famous English playwright in the world.

4. **star** [stɑr] *vt.* 主演

   · The movie, starring Julia Roberts, was a great hit.

5. **professor** [prə`fɛsɚ] *n.* [C] 教授

   · Ms. Carlson is a professor who teaches French at our college.

6. **murder** [`mɝdɚ] *n.* [U] 謀殺

   · The man was found guilty of murder.

7. **uncover** [ʌn`kʌvɚ] *vt.* 揭露，發現

   · Amy uncovered her husband's secret by accident.

8. **Christian** [`krɪstʃən] *adj.* 基督教的；*n.* [C] 基督徒

   · There is a Christian church in my neighborhood.

   · A Christian follows the religion based on the teachings of Jesus Christ.

9. **religion** [rɪ`lɪdʒən] *n.* [C] 宗教

   religious [rɪ`lɪdʒəs] *adj.* 宗教的

   · Do you believe in any religion?

   · The Mass is the religious ceremony of the Catholic Church.

10. **disappoint** [ˌdɪsə`pɔɪnt] *vt.* 使⋯失望

   · Your rude behavior really disappointed your parents.

11. **performance** [pɚ`fɔrməns] *n.* [C] 演出，表演

   · The band will give one more performance before leaving Taiwan.

12. **disrespectful** [ˌdɪsrɪ`spɛktfəl] *adj.* 不尊重的，無禮的

   · Many young people today are disrespectful to the elders.

13. **imply** [ɪm`plaɪ] *vt.* 暗示

   · Silence often implies that you agree with what others say.

14. **Catholic** [`kæθəlɪk] *adj.* 天主教的

   · The book has been banned by the Roman Catholic Church since 1935.

15. **denounce** [dɪ`naʊns] *vt.* 譴責

   · The mother who abused her kids was denounced by the whole society.

16. **ban** [bæn] *vt.* 禁止

- Smoking is banned indoors.

17. **strike** [straɪk] *n.* [C] 罷工

   · I had to take a taxi to the office this morning because the bus drivers went on strike.

18. **considerable** [kən`sɪdərəbḷ] *adj.* 相當 (多) 的

   · Paul has earned a considerable amount of money by investing in the stock market.

19. **conservative** [kən`sɜvətɪv] *adj.* 保守的

   · Diane is considered conservative because she dislikes changing.

20. **flock** [flɑk] *vi.* 成群地去

   · Young people flock to big cities in order to find better jobs.

21. **version** [`vɜʒən] *n.* [C] 版本

   · It's easy to get a Chinese version of this English novel because it is very popular.

Idioms & Phrases

1. **cover up**　掩蓋，掩飾

   · Once you tell a lie, you have to tell more to cover it up.

2. **see for oneself**　眼見為憑

   · If you don't believe that your brother bought a new car, go and see for yourself.

Pop Quiz

Fill in each blank with the answer that matches the definition.

(A) professor	(B) definitely	(C) imply	(D) conservative
(E) Catholic	(F) uncover	(G) strike	(H) flock
(I) cover up	(J) see for oneself		

_____ 1. to find out something secret

_____ 2. traditional and not liking changing

_____ 3. a period of time when some workers stop working mainly because they ask for better pay or working conditions

_____ 4. to prevent others from knowing one's mistakes or the truth about something

_____ 5. certainly and without any doubt

UNIT 08

Dangers of [1]MP3 Players

October, 2006

It seems as if everyone today has an MP3 player. Young people **in particular** can frequently be seen listening to their favorite songs on these portable music players while walking to class, taking the subway, or exercising in a gym. **Without a doubt**, MP3 players are popular, but new research suggests that they may not be so good for our ears. In fact, listening to an MP3 player can affect a listener's hearing and may even eventually cause deafness.

A recent survey in the [2]United Kingdom discovered that **more and more** young people use MP3 players. In the survey, 14 percent of people admitted spending as much as 28 hours each week listening to their MP3 players. Some even said that they suffered from ringing in the ears, which is a sure sign of damage to their hearing. However, these people said that they continued using their MP3 players every day.

An American specialist in the science of hearing has also warned of the dangers of MP3 devices. Damage to a person's hearing usually occurs if the noise level exceeds 85 decibels for a long period of time. Unfortunately, many people listen to their MP3 players at levels that exceed 85 decibels, especially when they **work out**. Not only is this bad for a person's hearing but it may also be dangerous to others, particularly if the person is jogging or riding a scooter.

In Hong Kong, a hearing specialist has also raised concern about the popular practice of listening to an MP3 player while people take the subway. Since it is already very noisy on the subway, MP3 listeners must **turn up** their players to even higher levels to hear their music clearly. This, however, could cause hearing damage or even hearing loss to occur more quickly.

Therefore, **turn down** the volume on your MP3 player the next time you listen to it, or at least be aware of the possible risks. Actually, great care should always be taken whenever you use headphones. Other people should not be able to hear the music that you are listening to—if they can, it is too loud. Or you can choose not to use headphones at all when you listen to music in order to protect your ears. **After all**, hearing loss is preventable. As the old saying goes, "An ounce of prevention is worth a pound of cure." So, if you don't take great care when listening to an MP3 player now, you might not be able to enjoy listening to your favorite songs—or anything at all—in the future.

Reading Comprehension

Choose the best answers.

(　　) 1. This passage mainly talks about _____ .

    (A) where to buy the best MP3 player

    (B) when to use the headphones while listening to music

    (C) how to listen to an MP3 player when we ride a scooter

    (D) what may happen to our hearing if we don't take care when listening to an MP3 player

(　　) 2. Which of the following statements about the survey in the United Kingdom is NOT true?

    (A) In the survey, some people suffered from hearing damage.

    (B) In the survey, more and more young people like to listen to MP3 players.

    (C) In the survey, 14 percent of people spent more than 28 hours listening to MP3 players a week.

    (D) In the survey, people who suffered from ringing in the ears didn't listen to MP3 players anymore.

(　　) 3. Why may listening to MP3 players cause loss of hearing?

    (A) The MP3 devices are always portable.

    (B) The headphones are convenient to use.

    (C) The volume on MP3 players is often too high.

    (D) The music level on MP3 players is usually below 85 decibels.

(　　) 4. Which of the following proverbs has the similar idea to that of "an ounce of prevention is worth a pound of cure"?

    (A) A stitch in time saves nine.

    (B) A kite rises against the wind.

    (C) The early bird catches the worm.

    (D) A picture is worth a thousand words.

(   ) 5. We should _____ when we listen to an MP3 player.

      (A) always use the headphones

      (B) be aware of the possible risks

      (C) only listen to our favorite songs

      (D) let other people also listen to the music

Vocabulary

1. **frequently** [ˋfrikwəntlɪ] *adv.* 經常地
   - Peggy goes to the café so frequently that the waiter knows what she likes to drink.

2. **portable** [ˋportəbl̩] *adj.* 便於攜帶的
   - Bill carried a portable computer and wrote his novel whenever he had free time.

3. **survey** [ˋsɝve] *n.* [C] 調查
   - The survey showed that most people spent at least three hours a day watching TV.

4. **admit** [ədˋmɪt] *vt.* 承認
   - The boy admitted stealing the MP3 player from the store.

5. **suffer** [ˋsʌfɚ] *vi.* 受苦，患病
   - Frank has suffered from high blood pressure for many years.

6. **specialist** [ˋspɛʃəlɪst] *n.* [C] 專家
   - Mr. Lee is a bird specialist; he has studied birds for more than twenty years.

7. **warn** [wɔrn] *vt.* 警告
   - Our teacher warned us not to do anything against the law.

8. **device** [dɪˋvaɪs] *n.* [C] 裝置
   - This ballpoint pen is a new device for recording sounds.

9. **exceed** [ɪkˋsid] *vt.* 超過
   - I couldn't afford the car because its price exceeded 800,000 NT dollars.

10. **decibel** [ˋdɛsəˌbɛl] *n.* [C] 分貝 (聲音強度單位)
    - The sound in the club, which is surely above 80 decibels, may be harmful to your ears if you stay too long.

11. **scooter** [ˋskutɚ] *n.* [C] 小型摩托車
    - We rented a scooter to go around the small island.

12. **volume** [ˋvɑljəm] *n.* [U] 音量

· Please turn down the volume on the radio; the baby is asleep.

13. **aware** [əˋwɛr] *adj.* 意識到的，知道的

· In the darkness, Jennifer was still aware of someone getting close to her.

14. **ounce** [aʊns] *n.* [C] 盎斯 (重量單位)

· One ounce is equal to about 28 grams.

15. **prevention** [prɪˋvɛnʃən] *n.* [U] 預防

· Much attention has been given to fire prevention after the forest fire.

Idioms & Phrases

1. **in particular**　特別地，尤其

· The man owes his success to many people, his wife in particular.

2. **without a doubt**　無疑地

· Ted is without a doubt the most intelligent boy in our class.

3. **more and more**　越來越多的

· Nowadays, more and more people have become vegetarians for health reasons.

4. **work out**　健身

· Jim works out at the gym three times a week.

5. **turn up**　調高 (音量)

· I can't hear the news on the radio clearly. Would you please turn the volume up?

6. **turn down**　調低 (音量)

· Turn the TV down; I am studying.

7. **after all**　畢竟

· Don't blame everything on Johnny! After all, he's only a kid.

Pop Quiz

Fill in each blank with the antonym (反義字).

(A) deny	(B) turn up	(C) ignorant	(D) seldom	(E) risk
(F) less and less	(G) after all	(H) survey	(I) fixed	(J) device

_____ 1. frequently

_____ 2. more and more

_____ 3. admit

_____ 4. portable

_____ 5. turn down

_____ 6. aware

UNIT 09

[1] *Guanghua Market Relocates*

February, 2006

For many years, Guanghua Market has always been the place for people to find and buy cheap computer and electronic items. Bargain hunters, both young and old, regularly packed the crowded market as they shopped for computers, computer parts and hardware, digital cameras, MP3 players, and other electronic goods. Those interested in used books also went to Guanghua Market, since this market also housed the largest group of second-hand booksellers in northern Taiwan. Now, the Taipei City Government has decided to close the market and relocate it to an area nearby.

The decision to **tear down** the Guanghua overpass was made mostly because of safety concerns. Guanghua Market had been located under an overhead highway for more than thirty years. Nevertheless, in recent years, the problem about the safety of the market, especially after a major earthquake, became serious. As a result, the government decided to move it to a temporary location, while a new permanent building for the market is being built on Xinsheng South Road.

Opened in the spring of 1973, Guanghua Market was originally intended for second-hand book retailers. **Later on**, jade and antique sellers also began to do business there. In the 80s, as computer and electronics manufacturing began to grow in Taiwan, the retailers in the market started to sell electronic parts and equipment. Guanghua's popularity gradually grew, mainly because fierce competition among the stores always kept the prices very low.

The new permanent Guanghua Market is scheduled to be completed in February of 2007. However, some Taipei residents said that they would still miss the old, busy, and crowded Guanghua, and the bargains—and memories—they found there.

Choose the best answers.

(　　) 1. When was Guanghua Market opened?

    (A) In the fall of 1973.　　　　　(B) In February of 2000.

    (C) In the spring of 1973.　　　　(D) In January of 2006.

(　　) 2. What products are mainly sold in Guanghua Market nowadays?

    (A) Food.　　　　　　　　　　　(B) Flowers.

    (C) Antiques.　　　　　　　　　(D) Electronic goods.

(　　) 3. Why did the Taipei City Government decide to relocate Guanghua Market?

    (A) It was mainly because of safety concerns.

    (B) A major earthquake once hit this place and caused damage to it.

    (C) The market has been located under an overhead highway for more than thirty years.

    (D) All of the above.

(　　) 4. What made the stores in Guanghua Market keep the prices of their goods low?

    (A) Because the market was old and crowded.

    (B) Because jade and antique sellers also did business there.

    (C) Because there was fierce competition among the stores.

    (D) Because the sellers had to sell out all their goods before the market was relocated.

(　　) 5. Which of the following statements is NOT true?

    (A) The safety of the market has been questioned seriously these years.

    (B) People would still miss the old, busy, and crowded Guanghua Market.

    (C) People can find many cheap and high-quality clothing in the new Guanghua Market.

    (D) Guanghua Market is the biggest second-hand book market in northern Taiwan.

Vocabulary

1. **relocate** [rɪˋloket] *vi.* 遷移到新地點
   · The Smiths relocated to New York City three months ago.

2. **electronic** [ɪˌlɛkˋtrɑnɪk] *adj.* 電子的
   electronics [ɪˌlɛkˋtrɑnɪks] *n.* [U] 電子設備
   · This electronic device is designed to make hot coffee.
   · The electronics company closed down because of economic depression.

3. **bargain** [ˋbɑrgɪn] *n.* [C] 特價品
   · This pair of shoes is really a bargain.

4. **hardware** [ˋhɑrdˌwɛr] *n.* [U] 硬體 (設備)
   · Let's go to Guanghua Market to buy some computer hardware.

5. **digital** [ˋdɪdʒɪtl̩] *adj.* 數位的
   · Digital cameras are popular because the pictures can be edited on computers.

6. **goods** [gʊdz] *n.* (*pl.*) 商品，貨物
   · You can find lots of goods in low prices in the flea market.

7. **house** [haʊz] *vt.* 容納
   · The big hotel is able to house more than 2,000 guests.

8. **nevertheless** [ˌnɛvɚðəˋlɛs] *adv.* 然而
   · May was told to stay at home, but she went to the movies nevertheless.

9. **temporary** [ˋtɛmpəˌrɛrɪ] *adj.* 臨時的
   · Many students like to find a temporary job during the summer vacation.

10. **permanent** [ˋpɝmənənt] *adj.* 永久的
    · Rachel lives in Taipei temporarily, and her permanent address is in Taichung.

11. **originally** [əˋrɪdʒənl̩ɪ] *adv.* 原本地，最初地
    · Originally, this big city was only a small seaport.

12. **intend** [ɪnˋtɛnd] *vt.* 預定
    · This gift is intended for my best friend.

13. **retailer** [ˋritelɚ] *n.* [C] 零售商
    · Mr. Chen has been a toy retailer for more than twenty years.

14. **jade** [dʒed] *n.* [U] 玉
    · My mother has a very beautiful jade necklace.

15. **antique** [ænˋtik] *n.* [C] 古董，古玩
   · The rich man spent millions of dollars on antiques.

16. **manufacturing** [ˌmænjəˋfæktʃərɪŋ] *n.* [U] 製造業
   · Taiwan is famous for its electronic manufacturing.

17. **equipment** [ɪˋkwɪpmənt] *n.* [U] 配備，設備
   · A computer is the necessary piece of equipment for a college student.

18. **gradually** [ˋgrædʒʊəlɪ] *adv.* 逐漸地
   · After the doctor's treatment, my knee gradually got better.

19. **schedule** [ˋskɛdʒʊl] *vt.* 安排，預定
   · We are scheduled to leave for Japan next Monday.

20. **resident** [ˋrɛzədənt] *n.* [C] 居民
   · The residents here are unhappy about the increasing number of visitors.

Idioms & Phrases

1. **tear down**   拆除 (建築物等)
   · The old building was torn down after the strong earthquake.

2. **later on**   之後
   · Molly refused to go to the party at first, but later on, she changed her mind.

Pop Quiz

Choose the best answer to each of the following sentences.

(   ) 1. They built a _____ library for use before the new one was completed.
   (A) permanent   (B) digital   (C) temporary   (D) definite

(   ) 2. This book we are editing is _____ for college students.
   (A) concerned   (B) housed   (C) torn   (D) intended

(   ) 3. _____, my father didn't like my pet cat. Now he sees it as a part of the family.
   (A) Gradually   (B) Originally   (C) Mainly   (D) Actually

(   ) 4. There is a store selling high-tech fishing _____ near my house.
   (A) equipment   (B) memory   (C) jade   (D) retailer

(   ) 5. Mr. Li plans to _____ his old house and build a new apartment for his family.
   (A) put off   (B) tear down   (C) tell apart   (D) take away

UNIT 10

[1]Heath Ledger: Dead at the Age of 28

February, 2008

The world lost one of its most promising young actors in late January. Heath Ledger, the star of [2]*Brokeback Mountain*, was found dead in New York City on January 22. The exact cause of his death, however, still remains unknown at this time.

What is known is that Ledger was discovered in the bedroom of his apartment. He was found naked, lying face-down beside his bed. Prescription sleeping pills were also found nearby.

At first, Ledger's death was reported as a suicide. However, some medical experts now say that his death might have been accidental. They say that Ledger may have accidentally taken the wrong combination of prescription pills. No illegal drugs were found in his home.

Ledger first became a star in films such as [3]*The Patriot* and [4]*A Knight's Tale*. He later gained critical acclaim playing a gay cowboy in [5]Ang Lee's hit film *Brokeback Mountain*. Ledger received an [6]Oscar nomination for his performance in this film. After learning of Ledger's death, Lee stated that working with him had been "one of the purest joys of my life."

Sadly, Ledger died at a time when he was at the top of his career. He had just finished filming his part as the Joker in the soon-to-be released Batman movie *The Dark Knight*. Early reports said that this may have been his finest film performance yet. Ledger, however, had said that this role had been very demanding. In an interview weeks before his death, Ledger commented: "Last week I probably slept an average of two hours a night. I couldn't stop thinking. My body was exhausted, and my mind was still going."

Ledger is survived by his wife and young daughter. His body has been returned to his native Australia at the request of his family there, and he will be buried near his hometown of [7]Perth.

Choose the best answers.

(   ) 1. What is the exact cause of Heath Ledger's death?

      (A) He took too much sleeping pills at once.

      (B) He used illegal drugs.

      (C) He died when filming *Brokeback Mountain.*

      (D) We still don't know the exact cause of his death.

(   ) 2. Heath Ledger was _____ when he was found dead.

      (A) wearing nothing   (B) facing the sky

      (C) in his apartment in Australia   (D) lying on his bed

(   ) 3. Early reports said that Ledger may have given his finest film performance in

      _____ .

      (A) *The Dark Knight*   (B) *Brokeback Mountain*

      (C) *The Patriot*   (D) *A Knight's Tale*

(   ) 4. What does the word "**survived**" in the last paragraph mean?

      (A) To continue to live after an accident

      (B) To live longer than someone

      (C) To last for a period of time

      (D) To continue to be successful

(   ) 5. Heath Ledger was born in _____ .

      (A) Australia   (B) London

      (C) New York City   (D) Brokeback Mountain

Vocabulary

1. **promising** [`prɑmɪsɪŋ] *adj.* 有前途的

   · Ted is a promising young man because he is not only smart but diligent.

2. **remain** [rɪ`men] *vi.* 保持，持續

   · Please remain seated until your name is called.

3. **prescription** [`prɪ`skrɪpʃən] *n.* [C] 處方

   · You need to go to the pharmacy to fill this prescription.

4. **pill** [pɪl] *n.* [C] 藥丸

．Grace cannot fall asleep without taking sleeping pills.

5. **medical** [ˋmɛdɪkl̩] *adj.* 醫學的

　　．The patient refused any further medical treatment and died as a consequence.

6. **accidental** [͵æksəˋdɛntl̩] *adj.* 意外的

　　．The accidental success of Sarah's first album was beyond our expectations.

7. **combination** [͵kɑmbəˋneʃən] *n.* [C] 結合，聯合

　　．The young designer has the perfect combination of talent and creativity.

8. **acclaim** [əˋklem] *n.* [U] 讚揚，喝采

　　．The artist is very famous and his work has won international acclaim.

9. **gay** [ge] *adj.* （男）同性戀的

　　．The man deserves to be treated equally no matter he is gay or straight.

10. **nomination** [͵nɑməˋneʃən] *n.* [U] 提名

　　．The scientist's great discovery won him the nomination for the Nobel Prize in Chemistry.

11. **pure** [pjʊr] *adj.* 完全的，十足的

　　．The kid has shown his pure talent for music at the age of 5.

12. **career** [kəˋrɪr] *n.* [C] 事業

　　．I started my career as an editor in a publishing house in 1999.

13. **release** [rɪˋlis] *vt.* 發行

　　．Stephen Chou's new movie will be released later this year.

14. **demanding** [dɪˋmændɪŋ] *adj.* 要求很高的，吃力的

　　．It is demanding to work for my boss, who always wants the best of the best.

15. **comment** [ˋkɑmɛnt] *vt.* 評論

　　．Many critics commented that Ang Lee's new movie was the best of the year.

16. **exhausted** [ɪgˋzɔstɪd] *adj.* 精疲力竭的

　　．I was exhausted after having walked for six hours to get to the destination.

17. **native** [ˋnetɪv] *adj.* 出生地的

　　．Bobby was born in Hsinchu and his native language is Hakka.

18. **request** [rɪˋkwɛst] *n.* [C] 要求，請求

　　．The guest has made a request for a non-smoking double room.

19. **bury** [ˋbɛrɪ] *vt.* 埋葬

　　．Isaac Newton was buried in Westminster Abbey after he died in 1727.

20. **hometown** [`hom`taun] *n.* [C] 故鄉，家鄉

　· Judy missed the food of her hometown very much when studying abroad.

Idioms & Phrases

at first　起先

· At first, Fanny was shy, but she gradually shared her feelings and opinions with us.

Pop Quiz

Choose the answer that is closest in meaning with the underlined part.

(　　) 1. Because Tony didn't know what to say in the meeting, he sat still and <u>remained</u> silent.

　　　(A) kept　　　　(B) buried　　　　(C) broke　　　　(D) implied

(　　) 2. Some customers have made a <u>request</u> for more information about our new model of cell phone.

　　　(A) career　　　(B) code　　　　(C) demand　　　(D) exception

(　　) 3. Sophie's new novel has won great <u>acclaim</u> all over the world.

　　　(A) criticism　　(B) praise　　　(C) profession　　(D) information

(　　) 4. After receiving the flowers from her boyfriend, Karen gave him a big smile of <u>pure</u> joy.

　　　(A) aware　　　(B) accidental　　(C) outstanding　(D) complete

(　　) 5. <u>At first</u>, I thought Joe was a nice guy, but it turned out that he was a big liar.

　　　(A) Later on　　　　　　　(B) At once

　　　(C) In the beginning　　　　(D) In fact

UNIT 11

High-Speed Rail Debuts in Taiwan

February, 2007

In the beginning of 2007, the people of Taiwan saw the start of service on the island's newest and fastest railway—the [1]Taiwan High Speed Rail (THSR). Beginning in January of this year, trains traveling at speeds of 300 kilometers per hour started to carry passengers between Taipei and Kaohsiung, Taiwan's two largest cities. This journey, which takes four to six hours on the old railway, has now been **cut down** to only ninety minutes on the new high-speed trains.

Many hope that this new high-speed rail service will benefit Taiwan, especially the millions of people who live on the western side of the island, where the high-speed rail runs. One researcher predicted, "With the opening of the high-speed rail, Taiwan island will become Taiwan city." According to some experts, the THSR will allow "Taiwan city" to compete economically against other leading Asian cities, such as [2]Hong Kong and Shanghai, by decreasing travel time and costs, and by increasing communications between Taiwan's cities.

However, the high-speed rail project has also been controversial since the day it was first announced. Some have criticized the decision to switch from the European system first selected to Japanese "[3]bullet-train" technology. Others have cited reports of financial, safety, and construction problems as the line was being built. And the date for the opening of the THSR, originally scheduled for 2003, had to be **pushed back** several times for different reasons. Most recently, ticketing problems have upset many customers, who have been very dissatisfied with the inconvenience of reserving seats and buying tickets for the THSR.

Will the THSR really change the way people live, work, and travel in Taiwan? Right now, it is too soon to tell. However, with a price tag of US$15 billion, the Taiwan High Speed Rail is one investment that the people of Taiwan hope will **pay off** for the nation.

Choose the best answers.

(   ) 1. How would the THSR allow "Taiwan city" to compete against other leading
Asian cities?

(A) By increasing travel time and costs between Taiwan's cities.

(B) By decreasing communications between Taiwan's cities.

(C) By increasing communications between Taiwan's cities.

(D) By cutting down the time spent traveling between Taipei and Kaohsiung
to only four to six hours.

(   ) 2. Which of the following problems has upset many THSR customers?

(A) The speed of the train.   (B) The Japanese food on the trains.

(C) The seat reservation system.   (D) The train schedule.

(   ) 3. The passage mainly talks about _____ .

(A) the distance between Taiwan's cities

(B) how much it would cost to build a railway

(C) the differences between Taiwan city and other leading Asian cities

(D) the influence of the THSR system on Taiwan

(   ) 4. The THSR system _____ .

(A) is originally scheduled to open in 2007

(B) doesn't have problems regarding ticketing and seat reservation

(C) travels 300 kilometers per minute

(D) costs US$15 billion to build

(   ) 5. Which of the following statements is NOT true?

(A) The THSR started to run in January, 2007.

(B) The THSR has switched from the European system to the Japanese
system.

(C) People in Taiwan are all very satisfied with the THSR system.

(D) The THSR system might change the way people live in Taiwan.

Vocabulary

1. **rail** [rel] *n.* [U] 鐵路，鐵道
   · Traveling by rail is a convenient way to go around Taiwan.

2. **debut** [dɪ`bju] *vi.* 首次亮相
   · I am looking forward to seeing the magic show which will debut next month.

3. **benefit** [`bɛnəfɪt] *vt.* 使受益
   · If I won the lottery, I would use the money to do something that benefits others.

4. **predict** [prɪ`dɪkt] *vt.* 預言
   · No one believed the old woman when she said she could predict the future.

5. **economically** [ˌikə`nɑmɪklɪ] *adv.* 在經濟上
   · Todd has relied on his parents economically for months since he lost his job.

6. **decrease** [dɪ`kris] *vt.* 減少
   · We decreased the amount of water we used every day during the drought.

7. **communication** [kəˌmjunə`keʃən] *n.* [C] 運輸；[U] 通信，交流
   · The bridge improves the communications between the two villages.
   · I was still in communication with my friends in Taiwan when studying abroad.

8. **controversial** [ˌkɑntrə`vɝʃəl] *adj.* 有爭議的
   · Building a nuclear power plant in this village is a highly controversial plan.

9. **announce** [ə`naʊns] *vt.* 宣佈
   · Everyone was shocked when Joan announced that she's getting married next month.

10. **switch** [`swɪtʃ] *vi.* 改變，轉變
    · The excellent interpreter can switch between English and Chinese fluently.

11. **technology** [tɛk`nɑlədʒɪ] *n.* [U] 科技
    · With modern technology, we can do lots of things considered impossible in the past.

12. **cite** [saɪt] *vt.* 引用，舉出
    · The judge cited evidence to prove that the man was guilty.

13. **financial** [faɪ`nænʃəl] *adj.* 財務的，金融的
    · Recently lots of companies have gone out of business because of financial difficulties.

14. **construction** [kən`strʌkʃən] *n.* [U] 建造，施工
    · After the construction of the railroad is done, we can travel around the island by rail.

15. **upset** [ʌp`sɛt] *vt.* 使生氣（～, upset, upset)

- Tim's decision to go to law school upsets his parents; they want him to be a doctor.

16. **reserve** [rɪ`zɝv] *vt.* 預定，預約

   · I have reserved a table for two in the French restaurant tonight.

17. **billion** [`bɪljən] *n.* [C] 十億

   · There are more than six billion people on Earth.

18. **investment** [ɪn`vɛstmənt] *n.* [U] 投資

   · Joe's investment in the stock market made him lose most of his money.

Idioms & Phrases

1. **cut down**　縮短

   · Allen's mom asked him to cut down on the amount of time he spent on TV.

2. **push back**　延遲

   · The meeting was pushed back from 4 p.m. to 6 p.m. because the manager was late.

3. **pay off**　達到目的，獲得利益

   · If you work hard, your effort will finally pay off someday in the future.

Pop Quiz

Fill in each blank with the correct word or phrase to complete the passage. Make changes if necessary.

| predict | benefit | controversial | debut | switch |
| pay off | technology | communication | upset | financial |

　　Nowadays, the modern ¹_____, IM (instant messaging), has played an important role in many people's lives. Since IM is easy to use, faster than e-mail, and free, it has increased ²_____ between people all over the world. When IM first ³_____, people could only send simple black and white text messages. Now, people can send messages in many colors and sizes and they can also send funny pictures to show their emotions. Although IM is very popular with many computer users, it has become a highly ⁴_____ issue. Some employers complained and were ⁵_____ about it because their employees would chat with their friends online instead of focusing on their work in the offices.

UNIT 12

Horrible Hurricanes Hit ¹New Orleans, Louisiana

October, 2005

September has been a terrible month for many Americans. Over the last few weeks, two strong hurricanes had battered the Gulf Coast of the United States, and New Orleans in particular. These hurricanes not only left hundreds dead and thousands homeless, but also caused more than 100 billion dollars in damage.

The disaster began with ²Hurricane Katrina on August 29. At first, the damage did not seem so severe. However, in the days that followed, several levees broke. After that, New Orleans was almost completely flooded. In some places, the floodwaters reached 20 feet (6 meters), and the entire city was left without clean water or electricity for several days. Because the flooding was so extensive, many residents were stranded in their homes long after Hurricane Katrina had left. Some even climbed to their rooftops to escape the rising waters and await rescue. Experts said that the flooding caused by the hurricane was actually more destructive than the hurricane itself.

All in all, Hurricane Katrina caused more than 1,800 deaths and more than US$100 billion in damage, making it the most costly natural disaster in U.S. history. Although most government officials worked together to rescue people from the areas affected, many people criticized the national government for its sluggish response.

Unfortunately, the departure of Katrina was not the end of the tragedy. Another category 5 hurricane, ³Hurricane Rita, hit this devastated region on September 24 and caused parts of New Orleans to flood again.

Residents of New Orleans and the Gulf Coast hope that the worst of this hurricane season is now over. Many have now returned to their homes and begin the difficult process of picking up the pieces of their shattered lives.

Choose the best answers.

(   ) 1. The two hurricanes did NOT cause _____ .

(A) hundreds dead and thousands homeless

(B) billions of dollars in damage

(C) the rise of gold price

(D) the lack of clean water or electricity in New Orleans for several days

(   ) 2. From the passage, we can tell that a "**levee**" is _____ .

(A) a low wall built at the side of a river to prevent flooding

(B) a boat that can rescue people from flooding areas

(C) a place that supplies electricity to people

(D) the flooding caused by a hurricane

(   ) 3. Which of the following statements is NOT true?

(A) Hurricane Rita broke several levees.

(B) Two hurricanes hit the Gulf Coast and caused a great deal of damage.

(C) Some places near the Gulf Coast were flooded after the two hurricanes.

(D) Hurricane Katrina is the most costly natural disaster in U.S. history.

(   ) 4. The meaning of the word "**sluggish**" in the third paragraph is similar to

_____ .

(A) sad   (B) slow   (C) quick   (D) unfriendly

(   ) 5. Which of the following statements is true?

(A) After Katrina left, the tragedy was finally over.

(B) Many residents in New Orleans climbed to their rooftops to rescue others.

(C) People blamed the government for breaking the levees after Katrina had left.

(D) The flood caused by Hurricane Katrina was more damaging than the hurricane itself.

Vocabulary

1. **horrible** [`hɔrəbl] *adj.* 令人恐懼的
   · Jimmy woke from a horrible nightmare at 4 a.m. and couldn't fall asleep anymore.

2. **hurricane** [`hɜɪ,ken] *n.* [C] 颶風
   · The strong hurricane destroyed a small village on the island.

3. **batter** [`bætɚ] *vt.* 搗毀，打碎
   · Hundreds of houses were battered by bombs during the war.

4. **levee** [`lɛvɪ] *n.* [C] 河堤
   · The government decided to build new levees along the riverside.

5. **floodwater** [``flʌdwɔtɚ] *n.* (*usu. pl.*) 洪水
   · In the Bible story, Noah built an ark to save many animals from the floodwaters.

6. **stranded** [`strændɪd] *adj.* 受困的
   · The typhoon kept us stranded at the airport for a whole day.

7. **rooftop** [`ruf,tɑp] *n.* [C] 屋頂
   · Jason climbed to the rooftop in order to fix the hole on it.

8. **escape** [ə`skep] *vt.* 逃脫
   · The boy escaped punishment by telling a lie to his parents.

9. **await** [ə`wet] *vt.* 等待
   · Buck's mother was awaiting him at home when he returned late at night.

10. **rescue** [`rɛskju] *n.* [U] 救援
    · The dog is trained to come to a person's rescue when he or she needs help.

11. **destructive** [dɪ`strʌktɪv] *adj.* 破壞性的
    · An earthquake is a kind of destructive force of nature.

12. **sluggish** [`slʌgɪʃ] *adj.* 遲緩的
    · Mrs. Johnson's movements become sluggish because of her illness.

13. **response** [rɪ`spɑns] *n.* [U] 反應，回應
    · Paul nodded in response to his father's question.

14. **unfortunately** [ʌn`fɔrtʃənɪtlɪ] *adv.* 不幸地
    · Unfortunately, Vicky missed the school bus and was late for school.

15. **departure** [dɪ`partʃɚ] *n.* [U] 離去
    · Our departure for Tainan was delayed by a severe typhoon.

16. **tragedy** [`trædʒədɪ] *n.* [C] 悲劇事件
    · It was a tragedy that the man shot 10 people and then committed suicide.
17. **category** [`kætə,gorɪ] *n.* [C] 等級，類別
    · Hurricane Katrina as well as Hurricane Rita is a category 5 hurricane.
18. **devastate** [`dɛvəs,tet] *vt.* 摧殘，破壞
    · The beautiful city was devastated by bomb attacks.
19. **shatter** [`ʃætɚ] *vt.* 毀壞，損壞
    · After the horrible earthquake, our house was completely shattered.

Idioms & Phrases

all in all　整體而言
· All in all, I think the ballerina's performance is very marvelous.

Pop Quiz

Choose the best answer to each of the following sentences.

(　　) 1. _____, Rita failed the math exam although she had prepared for it for weeks.
     (A) Sluggishly　　(B) Economically　(C) Unfortunately　(D) Luckily

(　　) 2. The Lins went to France to _____ the hot and humid summer in Taiwan.
     (A) rescue　　　(B) shatter　　　(C) escape　　　(D) batter

(　　) 3. When the teacher finished his jokes, there was no _____ from his students.
     (A) response　　(B) tragedy　　　(C) expert　　　(D) levee

(　　) 4. Jason was _____ on a mountain road because his car suddenly broke down.
     (A) devastated　(B) shattered　　(C) battered　　(D) stranded

(　　) 5. The _____ of the flight was delayed because of a violent storm.
     (A) flood　　　　(B) departure　　(C) category　　(D) process

UNIT 13

Million Dollar Baby KO's The Aviator at 2005 Oscars

March, 2005

Though there was a new host at this year's Academy Awards, there were few surprises, as most of the predicted favorites **ended up** winning Oscars.

The biggest success of the night was *Million Dollar Baby*. This film about a female boxer not only won the award for best picture but also the best director award for [1]Clint Eastwood. [2]Hilary Swank, who portrayed the boxer in the movie, won the Oscar for best actress. This was Swank's second Academy Award; she won her first in 2000. Morgan Freeman, who played an elderly ex-fighter in the film, **picked up** a best supporting actor award.

The Aviator did not do as well as many had expected. This big-budget film told the story of the eccentric billionaire [3]Howard Hughes, and it featured the popular actor Leonardo DiCaprio in the leading role. Though the film received eleven Academy Award nominations, it managed to win only five, including best supporting actress for Cate Blanchett. Perhaps most disappointingly, *The Aviator* failed to win the award for best picture and best director. Its director, [4]Martin Scorsese, failed to win an Oscar for the fifth time.

[5]Jamie Foxx, a former stand-up comedian, won the best actor award for his performance as the singer [6]Ray Charles in the movie *Ray*. In his acceptance speech, Foxx thanked his deceased grandmother for her guidance while he was growing up.

Altogether, an estimated 70 million people in the United States **tuned in to** watch all or part of this year's Oscars.

Choose the best answers.

(   ) 1. Why weren't there many surprises at this year's Oscars?

        (A) Because there wasn't a new host this year.

        (B) Because most of the predicted favorites won.

        (C) Because few people watched the show.

        (D) Because *The Aviator* won many awards.

(   ) 2. Who won the award for best director?

        (A) Martin Scorsese.   (B) Cate Blanchett.

        (C) Clint Eastwood.   (D) Morgan Freeman.

(   ) 3. Which of the following statements about Jamie Foxx is NOT true?

        (A) He was a comedian before.

        (B) He portrayed the singer Ray Charles in the film *Ray*.

        (C) He won the best actor award at this year's Oscars.

        (D) His grandmother was also there to see him receive the award.

(   ) 4. *The Aviator* did not do well at this year's Oscars because _____ .

        (A) it only won the best director award

        (B) Leonardo DiCaprio did not win the best supporting actor award

        (C) it only won five Oscars in total

        (D) the budget of the film was not enough

(   ) 5. What was the movie *Million Dollar Baby* about?

        (A) It was about the story of the director Clint Eastwood.

        (B) It was about a black singer.

        (C) It was a movie about airplanes.

        (D) It was about the story of a female boxer.

Vocabulary

1. **KO** [`ke`o] *vt.* (拳擊的) 擊倒，打倒
   · The short boxer KO'd his opponent beyond our expectations.

2. **aviator** [`evɪ,etɚ] *n.* [C] 飛行員，飛機駕駛員
   · The aviator fulfilled his dream of flying through the continent.

3. **Academy Award** [ə`kædəmɪ ə`wɔrd] *n.* [C] 影藝學院獎 (俗稱的奧斯卡獎)
   · Receiving an Academy Award is considered the highest honor in Hollywood.

4. **boxer** [`bɑksɚ] *n.* [C] 拳擊手
   · After making so much effort, the boxer finally became the world champion.

5. **portray** [por`tre] *vt.* 飾演
   · In the thriller, *The Silence of the Lambs*, Anthony Hopkins portrays a serial killer.

6. **elderly** [`ɛldɚlɪ] *adj.* 較年長的
   · I'm the fifth child and have four elderly sisters in my family.

7. **budget** [`bʌdʒɪt] *n.* [C] 經費；預算
   · Paula wants to go abroad for a vacation, but she doesn't have the budget for it.

8. **eccentric** [ɪk`sɛntrɪk] *adj.* 乖僻的，古怪的
   · After his wife died, Mr. Wang became an eccentric old man.

9. **feature** [`fitʃɚ] *vt.* 由…主演
   · *The Curious Case of Benjamin Button* features my favorite actor, Brad Pitt.

10. **manage** [`mænɪdʒ] *vt.* 設法做到
    · It was not easy, but finally we managed to get the job done.

11. **disappointingly** [,dɪsə`pɔɪntɪŋlɪ] *adv.* 令人失望地
    · Disappointingly, Daniel didn't show up at my birthday party as he had promised.

12. **stand-up** [`stænd,ʌp] *adj.* (喜劇演員) 在舞台上獨演的
    · The humorous stand-up comedian made the audience roll in the aisles.

13. **comedian** [kə`midɪən] *n.* [C] 喜劇演員
    · The popular comedian always brings a lot of laughter and joy to people around the world.

14. **acceptance** [ək`sɛptəns] *n.* [U] 領受
    · You should write a letter of thanks with the acceptance of a present from anyone.

15. **deceased** [dɪ`sist] *adj.* 已故的，死亡的

・ When Danny missed his deceased grandmother, he would look at her photos.

16. **guidance** [`gaɪdn̩s] *n.* [U] 指導，引導

　　・ Flora and her husband went to a counselor for guidance on their marriage.

17. **estimated** [`ɛstə,metɪd] *adj.* 估計的，大約的

　　・ The president wanted to know the estimated damage caused by the earthquake.

Idioms & Phrases

1. **end up**　結束

　　・ If you keep gambling, you will definitely end up losing all your money.

2. **pick up**　獲得

　　・ I picked up some writing skills when I was at college.

3. **tune in to**　調整 (電視，收音機) 至某台

　　・ I tuned in to the weather report to see if it would rain today.

Pop Quiz

Choose the answer that matches the definition.

(　　) 1. A(n) _____ person means someone who is dead.

　　(A) eccentric　　(B) deceased　　(C) elderly　　(D) stranded

(　　) 2. When you have a _____ for a program, it means you have a certain amount
of money available to use while carrying out the program.

　　(A) award　　(B) nomination　　(C) guidance　　(D) budget

(　　) 3. _____ means advice that is given to someone about what he/she should do.

　　(A) Acceptance　　(B) Appearance　　(C) Guidance　　(D) Academy

(　　) 4. When people say you _____ things quickly, it means that you learn fast.

　　(A) end up　　(B) turn up　　(C) pick up　　(D) grow up

(　　) 5. When people _____ to do something, it means they succeed in doing
something difficult.

　　(A) manage　　(B) portray　　(C) feature　　(D) estimate

UNIT 14

"Mom"—the Most Beautiful Word in English

January, 2005

What are your favorite words in English? Which English word do you think is the most beautiful? The [1]British Council, an organization that promotes British culture and English learning around the world, decided to find out what the most popular and best-loved words in English are. So, the Council conducted a survey and asked 40,000 people in 102 non-English speaking countries to name their favorite English words.

Recently, the British Council has published the results in a list of the world's 70 favorite English words. According to the survey, "mother" is the most popular word in the English language. Interestingly, the word "father" did not even make the list. Other English words that people around the world like are "passion," "smile," "love," and "eternity." An official from the British Council commented that the top words on the list were all strong and positive.

And the list had some surprises. Some of the unusual words that made the list included "peekaboo," "flabbergasted," "kangaroo,"and "oi." Literary words, such as "serendipity," "renaissance," and "loquacious," were also popular. And, of course, a few slang words, such as "oops" and "smashing," were mentioned.

The survey showed how quickly words can become popular in English. "Flip-flop," the fifty-ninth most popular word on the list, only has begun to be widely used in recent years. This word gained popularity during the 2004 U.S. presidential election, when [2]Republicans accused the [3]Democratic presidential candidate [4]John Kerry of having "flip-flopped"—or changed his position—on many issues.

The British Council carried out the survey of the world's 70 most beautiful English words to celebrate its seventieth anniversary.

Choose the best answers.

(　　) 1. According to the British Council's survey, "**mother**" is _____ .

(A) the most unusual English word to non-English speakers

(B) the most surprising English word to English speakers

(C) the favorite English word of non-English speakers

(D) the simplest word for non-English speakers

(　　) 2. Which of the following statements is NOT true?

(A) The word "oops" is one of the popular slang words in English.

(B) The word "oi" is one of the popular and common words in English.

(C) There were some surprises on the list of the world's 70 favorite English words.

(D) The top words on the list of the favorite English words are all positive.

(　　) 3. The word "**loquacious**" is a(n) _____ word.

(A) literary   (B) interesting

(C) positive   (D) common

(　　) 4. The British Council did NOT _____ .

(A) conduct a survey to find out what the most popular English words are

(B) ask 40,000 people in 102 non-English speaking countries to name their favorite English words

(C) refuse to publish the results of the survey

(D) organize the survey to celebrate its seventieth anniversary

(　　) 5. The passage infers that the word "**flip-flop**" _____ .

(A) is the forty-ninth most popular English word

(B) means that a person never changes his or her position on an issue

(C) was first used by the Democratic presidential candidate

(D) gained popularity during the 2004 U.S. presidential election

1. **promote** [prə`mot] *vt.* 推廣，促進
   · The city government is promoting the use of the new public transportation.

2. **conduct** [kən`dʌkt] *vt.* 進行
   · Joseph conducted an experiment in his biology class.

3. **passion** [`pæʃən] *n.* [U] 熱情
   · The poet expressed his passion for the lady by writing a love poem.

4. **eternity** [ɪ`tɜ˞nətɪ] *n.* [U] 永恆
   · On the wedding ceremony, Matt told his wife that he would love her for eternity.

5. **unusual** [ʌn`juʒʊəl] *adj.* 不尋常的，奇特的
   · It is unusual for Jessica to yell so loudly; she must be very angry.

6. **peekaboo** [`pikə,bu] *n.* [U] 躲貓貓 (將臉一隱一現逗小孩的遊戲)
   · Mrs. Davis liked to play peekaboo to entertain her little grandson.

7. **flabbergasted** [`flæbə˞,gæstɪd] *adj.* 目瞪口呆的，非常驚訝的
   · When the clerk told me the price of the watch, I was totally flabbergasted.

8. **kangaroo** [,kæŋgə`ru] *n.* [C] 袋鼠
   · When you travel in Australia, don't forget to see the cute kangaroos.

9. **oi** [ɔɪ] *interj.* 喂
   · Mr. Johnson yelled "Oi!" to the kid when seeing him stealing the candy.

10. **literary** [`lɪtə,rɛrɪ] *adj.* 文學 (上) 的
    · The writer's new novel has won many literary prizes.

11. **serendipity** [,sɛrən`dɪpətɪ] *n.* [U] 意外驚喜
    · The word "serendipity" means finding something useful or valuable unexpectedly.

12. **renaissance** [,rɛnə`zɑns] *n. (sing.)* 復興；重新流行
    · Jazz is enjoying a renaissance in the United States now.

13. **loquacious** [lo`kweʃəs] *adj.* 多話的
    · Loquacious students may disturb the order in class.

14. **slang** [slæŋ] *n.* [U] 俚語
    · When people chat online, they tend to use the Internet slang words.

15. **oops** [ups] *interj.* 哎喲，哎唷
    · When Bill accidentally stepped on my toes, he said, "Oops, sorry about that."

16. **smashing** [`smæʃɪŋ] *adj.* 十分出色的
   · Ivy looked smashing in the pink dress and caught everyone's attention at the party.
17. **flip-flop** [`flɪp,flɑp] *vi.* (立場) 反覆
   · We don't know exactly why Angela flip-flopped on this important issue.
18. **presidential** [,prɛzə`dɛnʃəl] *adj.* 總統的
   · In Taiwan, presidential elections are held every four years.
19. **election** [ɪ`lɛkʃən] *n.* [C] 選舉
   · Mr. Obama won the election and became the president of the United States.
20. **accuse** [ə`kjuz] *vt.* 譴責，指責
   · The mother believed her son and didn't accuse him of telling lies.
21. **candidate** [`kændədet] *n.* [C] 候選人
   · Mr. Jackson is one of the candidates running for mayor.
22. **issue** [`ɪʃju] *n.* [C] 議題
   · The pollution problem is the issue that will be discussed in the meeting.
23. **anniversary** [,ænə`vɝsərɪ] *n.* [C] (結婚) 週年紀念
   · My parents took a trip to Japan to celebrate their 20th anniversary.

Pop Quiz

Choose the best answer to each of the following sentences.

(   ) 1. Nancy and her husband will celebrate their first wedding _____ by having a candlelit dinner in the restaurant.
   (A) eternity   (B) election   (C) passion   (D) anniversary
(   ) 2. The company gave away free samples to _____ their new instant noodles.
   (A) promote   (B) conduct   (C) smash   (D) regulate
(   ) 3. "Airhead" is a(n) _____ for "a stupid person."
   (A) renaissance   (B) election   (C) peekaboo   (D) slang
(   ) 4. Ted is _____ and he can keep on talking without taking a rest for two hours.
   (A) smashing   (B) loquacious   (C) presidential   (D) literary
(   ) 5. Debbie was _____ when finding all the money in her purse was gone.
   (A) unusual   (B) passionate   (C) flabbergasted   (D) diligent

UNIT 15

¹Obama Makes History

December, 2008

History was made in America this fall when Barack Obama was elected the forty-fourth president of the United States. Obama is the first African American ever to hold this position. A Democrat, Obama defeated the Republican ²John McCain on November 5, as large numbers of Americans **turned out** to vote in this important election.

Barack Obama was born in Hawaii on August 4, 1961, to a black father from ³Kenya and a white mother from ⁴Kansas. His parents divorced a few years later. Obama's mother then remarried and moved the family to ⁵Indonesia, where Obama went to a public school until he turned ten. He was then brought back to Hawaii by his mother. A few years after graduating from ⁶Columbia University, Obama decided to move to Chicago, where he worked as a community organizer. He then went to ⁷Harvard Law School before becoming involved in politics.

As a junior senator from the State of ⁸Illinois, Obama remained unknown until he gave a speech at the Democratic National Convention in 2004. Called "The Audacity of Hope," this speech electrified the crowd and made Obama a national figure overnight. Many, however, were still surprised that he chose to **run for** the presidency three years later, since ⁹Hillary Clinton seemed the likely Democratic candidate at that time. Obama defeated Hillary in this primary race before going on to beat McCain in the general election this November.

When Obama's victory was announced, spontaneous celebrations erupted not only across the United States but also around the world, with people singing and dancing in the streets in ¹⁰Harlem and Kenya and even in a town called Obama in Japan. In Chicago, more than 300,000 people gathered to hear Obama speak. Many, including the TV star ¹¹Oprah Winfrey and the civil rights leader ¹²Jesse Jackson, were **in tears** as they celebrated this historic moment and listened to Obama speak.

In this speech, Obama was serious about challenges that America faces, calling them "the greatest of our lifetime—two wars, a planet in peril, the worst financial crisis in a century." However, just as he had done in his campaign,

Obama offered Americans—and the world—"hope" and "change." As Obama said that night: "In this election, at this **defining moment**, change has come to America."

Reading Comprehension

Choose the best answers.

(   ) 1. Why is the passage entitled "Obama Makes History?"

　　(A) Obama was the youngest senator ever from the State of Illinois.

　　(B) Obama became the first African-American president in American history.

　　(C) Obama was the first Hawaiian to study in Harvard Law School.

　　(D) Obama gave the most famous speech at the Democratic National Convention.

(   ) 2. Which of the following statements is NOT true about Barack Obama?

　　(A) He has a black father and a white mother.

　　(B) He went to a public school in Hawaii until he was ten.

　　(C) He graduated from Columbia University.

　　(D) He once worked as a community organizer in Chicago.

(   ) 3. By the year 2007, who was the most likely Democratic candidate in the next year's presidential election?

　　(A) John McCain.　　　　　　　　(B) Hillary Clinton.

　　(C) Oprah Winfrey.　　　　　　　(D) Jesse Jackson.

(   ) 4. About the celebrations of Obama's victory, which of the following is true?

　　(A) People sang and danced in the streets in a town called Obama in Kenya.

　　(B) In the United States, only people in Chicago celebrated his victory.

　　(C) In Hawaii, more than 300,000 people gathered to hear Obama speak.

　　(D) Many people were in tears as they celebrated this historic moment.

(   ) 5. According to this passage, we can infer that _____ .

　　(A) Jesse Jackson is a man fighting for African Americans' rights

　　(B) the world's economy has been very prosperous recently

　　(C) most people living in Harlem are white

　　(D) Obama has lived in Japan for a long time

1. **defeat** [dɪ`fit] *vt.* 擊敗
   · Richard was never defeated by failure because he was a person of strong will.

2. **divorce** [də`vors] *vi.* 離婚
   · Since Jessica's parents divorced, she has lived with her mother in Chicago.

3. **community** [kə`mjunətɪ] *n.* [C] 社區
   · Jack knows everyone in this community because he has lived here for years.

4. **organizer** [`ɔrgə,naɪzɚ] *n.* [C] 組織者
   · The success of the exhibition should be attributed to its talented organizer, Ruby.

5. **involved** [ɪn`vɑlvd] *adj.* 參與的
   · Our teacher encouraged us to get involved in some extracurricular activities.

6. **politics** [`pɑlə,tɪks] *n.* [U] 政治
   · "Politics is more difficult than physics," Einstein once said.

7. **senator** [`sɛnətɚ] *n.* [C] 參議員
   · Obama was a senator from Illinois before he was elected president in 2008.

8. **audacity** [ɔ`dæsətɪ] *n.* [U] 無畏，大膽
   · It sometimes needs audacity to stand up and fight for one's own rights.

9. **electrify** [ɪ`lɛktrə,faɪ] *vt.* 使震驚，使激動
   · The dancer's performance electrified us. We felt crazy about her after the show.

10. **overnight** [`ovɚ`naɪt] *adv.* 一夜之間；整夜
    · The singer's first album, which was a great hit, made him famous overnight.

11. **primary** [`praɪ,mɛrɪ] *adj.* 最初的，基層的
    · Joe finished primary school in 1985 and went to high school later that year.

12. **spontaneous** [spɑn`tenɪəs] *adj.* 自發的
    · Lily is a kind girl and is always spontaneous to help others.

13. **erupt** [ɪ`rʌpt] *vi.* 突然喧鬧起來
    · Everyone erupted in joy when the national baseball team won the gold medal.

14. **civil rights** [ˌsɪvl̩ `raɪts] *n.* (*pl.*) 公民權
    · Martin Luther King, Jr. was an important leader in the civil rights movement.

15. **challenge** [`tʃælɪndʒ] *n.* [C] 挑戰
    · Cathy is ready to meet the challenges of her new job.

16. **lifetime** [`laɪf,taɪm] *n.* [C] *(usu. sing.)* 一生，終生

　　· During his lifetime, Shakespeare wrote 38 plays and 154 sonnets.

17. **peril** [`pɛrəl] *n.* [U] 嚴重的危險

　　· The economic system in the United States is now in great peril.

18. **campaign** [kæm`pen] *n.* [C] 競選運動

　　· The presidential candidate invested lots of money in the campaign.

Idioms & Phrases

1. **turn out**　去參加

　　· Linda invited us to turn out to watch the school concert tomorrow night.

2. **run for**　競選

　　· The promising senator planned to run for the mayor of New York City.

3. **in tears**　哭泣

　　· Susan was in tears when reading this sad story about an orphan.

4. **defining moment**　關鍵時刻；決定性時刻

　　· The decision Dr. Lee made at that defining moment saved the boy's life.

Pop Quiz

Choose the best answer to each of the following sentences.

(　　) 1. Cathy is ready to meet the _____ of going to Harvard Law School.

　　　(A) company　　(B) challenge　　(C) campaign　　(D) community

(　　) 2. If we _____ the French team tonight, we will be in the finals.

　　　(A) defeat　　(B) define　　(C) display　　(D) depart

(　　) 3. After Dr. Smith finished his speech, there was a _____ burst of applause from the audience.

　　　(A) primary　　(B) historic　　(C) spontaneous　　(D) financial

(　　) 4. Since it was too late, I stayed at my cousin's house _____ and left for home the next day.

　　　(A) overall　　(B) lifetime　　(C) overnight　　(D) gradually

(　　) 5. Grace was _____ when she learned that she had failed the English exam.

　　　(A) in advance　　(B) all in all　　(C) in particular　　(D) in tears

UNIT 16

Postponed [1] *Hohaiyan Rock Festival Rocked Taiwan*

August, 2006

The Hohaiyan Rock Festival rocked Taiwan again. This year's festival was held over three days in [2]Fulong, Taipei County. Originally scheduled for the weekend of July 14, the rock festival had to be postponed because of [3]Tropical Storm Bilis. Luckily, the weather was better the following weekend, and the festival finished without a hitch before [4]Typhoon Kaemi could have any impact on the event.

For many years, the Hohaiyan Rock Festival has played an important role in introducing new music and new groups to the music scene in Taiwan. This year's Hohaiyan featured two stages for the fifty-four bands that had been invited to perform. A battle of the bands **took place** on Sunday, the last day of this year's Hohaiyan. This competition was considered to be the highlight of the festival. [5]Totem, last year's winner, performed this year. Other notable bands included the Chinese rock groups [6]Black Panther and [7]Tang Dynasty.

The festival was not without controversy, however. This year, Hohaiyan had a new organizer: [8]Formosa TV. Some fans and musicians complained that the new organizer made the festival into too much of a commercial event. Also, traffic was in chaos. After the festival had finished, the trip from Fulong back to Taipei took some people more than six hours.

Despite these problems, the 2006 Hohaiyan Rock Festival proved to be as popular as ever. Thousands of people had a wonderful weekend, relaxing on the beach and listening to great live music. Music fans hope that next year's festival will rock the island just as it did this year, and they also hope that the next Hohaiyan Rock Festival won't have to be postponed again because of bad weather!

Choose the best answers.

(　　) 1. What caused the 2006 Hohaiyan Rock Festival to be postponed?

    (A) Formosa TV.   (B) Typhoon Kaemi.

    (C) An old organizer.   (D) Tropical Storm Bilis.

(　　) 2. The word "**postponed**" in the first paragraph can be replaced by "＿＿＿＿."

    (A) canceled   (B) held later

    (C) first played   (D) done quickly

(　　) 3. Which of the following statements about this year's Rock Festival is NOT true?

    (A) The festival was supposed to take place on July 14.

    (B) There were 54 bands which were invited to perform.

    (C) During the festival, new music and new groups were introduced.

    (D) Totem was one of the new groups and also the winner of this year.

(　　) 4. Which of the following is NOT one of the problems of this year's festival?

    (A) The traffic.

    (B) The bad weather.

    (C) The competition of the bands.

    (D) The complaints about the new organizer.

(　　) 5. Which of the following words in the passage means "a small problem which causes a short delay"?

    (A) Hitch.   (B) Impact.

    (C) Controversy.   (D) Competition.

Vocabulary

1. **postpone** [post`pon] *vt.* 使延期，使延後

    · The baseball game was postponed until next Monday because of the heavy rain.

2. **hitch** [hɪtʃ] *n.* [C] (細微的) 障礙

    · After having prepared for three days, John passed the exam without a hitch.

3. **impact** [`ɪmpækt] *n.* [C] 影響，衝擊

    · New technology has made an impact on our lives.

4. **role** [rol] *n.* [C] 角色

· My sister played the role as the princess in the play.

5. **scene** [sin] *n.* [C] …界，活動領域；景色

· In the Taiwanese music scene, David Tao is one of the most popular singers.

· We went to the countryside and enjoyed the beautiful scene there.

6. **stage** [stedʒ] *n.* [C] 舞台；階段

· I have butterflies in my stomach whenever I have to speak on stage.

· Mary has shown her interest in singing at the early stage of her childhood.

7. **battle** [`bætl] *n.* [C] 爭鬥，戰鬥

· Most children in Africa often fight the battle against hunger.

8. **notable** [`notəbl̩] *adj.* 著名的

· The professor is notable for his wisdom and talent for math.

9. **commercial** [kə`mɝʃəl] *adj.* 營利的，商業性的；*n.* [C] 商業廣告

· The commercial success of the film made the originally unknown actor a superstar overnight.

· I don't like the TV show because it is always interrupted by commercials.

10. **chaos** [`keɑs] *n.* [U] 混亂

· Without a proper supply of electricity, the city was soon in chaos.

11. **relax** [rɪ`læks] *vi.* 放鬆

· After a busy day, I always relax by taking a hot bath and listening to some soft music.

12. **live** [laɪv] *adj.* 現場演出的

· We plan to listen to live music in the bar this Friday night.

Idioms & Phrases

take place 進行，發生

· Everyone was astonished when the terrible earthquake took place.

Fill in each blank with the correct word to complete the passage. Make changes if necessary.

impact	stage	scene	relax	hitch
commercial	notable	battle	role	chaos

We all have seen [1]_____, and we may even talk about the story or music used in them. However, something else also plays an important [2]_____ in commercials: color. A [3]_____ example is the color used in the commercials and advertisements for Coca-Cola. It is, of course, red. Studies have shown that red has a great [4]_____ on customers because it can attract their attention and looking at the color red makes them feel hungry and thirsty.

Green is another color often used in ads or commercials. Green is the color of nature and it makes people think of things that are natural, fresh, and pure. Looking at anything green can also make people [5]_____. So, color is surely a key element of a successful ad or commercial.

UNIT 17

Safety Concerns for [1]Maokong Gondola System

August, 2007

Maokong **used to** be Taipei's biggest tea-growing area, and with rolling green hills, winding hiking paths, and quiet teahouses, it has become one of the best places in Taiwan to experience authentic "tea culture." Recently, with the opening of the new Maokong Gondola system, it has also become much more convenient for visitors to explore this scenic spot.

The Maokong Gondola system began operation on July 4, 2007. At first, many people were excited, since the system is connected to Taipei's MRT at the Taipei Zoo Station, **making a visit to** Maokong very easy. The system has proved to be popular; more than 400,000 people have used it since its opening. Unfortunately, over the last month **or so**, some of the initial excitement about the new gondolas has turned into disappointment as a number of problems and mishaps have plagued the system.

To begin with, long lines greeted the opening of the gondolas, and since they did not have air conditioning, many passengers complained about the high temperatures inside. Then, only a few days after the start of operation, lightning caused the system to **shut down** for five hours, stranding hundreds of passengers in the air. In the weeks that followed, the gondolas were shut down again on numerous occasions because of malfunctions and equipment failure, leaving some people worried about the safety of the system.

In response to these concerns, the mayor of Taipei, [2]Hau Lung-bin (郝龍斌), has reassured the public that the Maokong Gondola is safe to ride. The [3]Taipei City Government has also announced that Maokong Gondola system will be closed every Monday so that regular safety inspections can be conducted.

It is hoped that all of these problems and issues will be worked out soon, since Maokong is definitely a beautiful place, and the Maokong Gondola system can provide visitors with a convenient—and scenic—way to visit it.

Choose the best answers.

(　　) 1. Which of the following statements about Maokong is NOT true?

    (A) It is one of the tourist attractions in Taipei.

    (B) It was the biggest tea-growing area in Taipei in the past.

    (C) People can experience tea culture in this place.

    (D) Few people visited this place before the opening of the gondola system.

(　　) 2. Which of the following was NOT the problem Maokong Gondola system met after it began operation?

    (A) Lack of tourists.   (B) Equipment failure.

    (C) High temperatures inside the car. (D) System breakdowns.

(　　) 3. The word "**plague**" in the second paragraph means "＿＿＿＿."

    (A) keeping one's popularity   (B) causing trouble

    (C) making something convenient   (D) spreading disease

(　　) 4. Which of the following about Maokong Gondola system is true?

    (A) It operates every day now.

    (B) Every gondola is equipped with an air conditioner.

    (C) It has been operating for more than a decade.

    (D) There are many concerns about its safety after it began operation.

(　　) 5. Which of the following statements is NOT true?

    (A) The mayor of Taipei assured people of the safety of Maokong Gondola system.

    (B) People are worrying about the safety of Maokong Gondola system.

    (C) Taipei Zoo Station makes a visit to Maokong more convenient.

    (D) A series of mishaps have disappointed people's expectations of Maokong Gondola system.

Vocabulary

1. **gondola** [ˋɡɑndələ] *n.* [C] (空中纜車的) 吊艙

  • I once rode the Maokong Gondola and enjoyed the view of the rolling hills there.

2. **system** [ˋsɪstəm] *n.* [C] 系統

· MRT Muzha Line introduced a system for dealing with emergencies to ensure safety.

3. **rolling** [ˋrolɪŋ] *adj.* (山丘等) 綿延起伏的

· The tour bus took us through the rolling hills to a national park.

4. **winding** [ˋwaɪndɪŋ] *adj.* 彎曲的，迂迴的

· The road leading to Mt. Ali is very long and winding.

5. **authentic** [ɔˋθɛntɪk] *adj.* 真正的，道地的

· The restaurant serves authentic Indian food that tastes really good.

6. **explore** [ɪkˋsplor] *vt.* 探索

· Japan has many interesting traditional cultures that many people love to explore.

7. **scenic** [ˋsinɪk] *adj.* 風景的

· We had a wonderful scenic tour of Eastern Taiwan last week.

8. **operation** [ˌɑpəˋreʃən] *n.* [U] 營運

· The new power plant will be in operation next week.

9. **connect** [kəˋnɛkt] *vt.* 連結

· The town is connected to Tainan City by train.

10. **disappointment** [ˌdɪsəˋpɔɪntmənt] *n.* [U] 失望

· To our disappointment, no rooms in this hotel were available.

11. **mishap** [ˋmɪsˌhæp] *n.* [C] 不幸事故，災難

· This mishap could have easily been avoided if Mary had not run the red light!

12. **plague** [pleg] *vt.* 使受到災禍

· The world has been plagued by environmental problems like global warming.

13. **air conditioning** [ˋɛr kənˋdɪʃənɪŋ] *n.* [U] 空調

· It was hot and everyone wanted to find a place with air conditioning to stay.

14. **strand** [strænd] *vt.* 使處於困境

· Thousands of the villagers were stranded in the mountains because of the typhoon.

15. **numerous** [ˋnjumərəs] *adj.* 很多的

· Numerous people died of Spanish Flu in 1918—more than World War I had killed.

16. **malfunction** [mælˋfʌŋkʃən] *n.* [C] 故障

· Due to the malfunction of the elevator, I had to walk up the stairs to the 12th floor.

17. **mayor** [ˋmeɚ] *n.* [C] 市長

· There will be four candidates running for the mayor's seat next year.

18. **reassure** [ˌriəˋʃʊr] *vt.* 再三保證

· The salesman reassured me that the price he offered was the lowest.

19. **inspection** [ɪn`spɛkʃən] *n.* [C] 檢查

  · The electric power company sent a man to my place to make a regular inspection.

Idioms & Phrases

1. **used to** 過去時常

  · I used to eat a lot of fast food, but now I don't eat junk food anymore.

2. **make a visit to** 參觀

  · We'll make a visit to the Museum of Modern Art this Saturday.

3. **or so** 大約

  · Jane spent ten thousand NT dollars or so on clothes and boots last month.

4. **to begin with** 首先

  · A: Why are you so angry with Marie?

  B: Well, to begin with, she laughed at my hairstyle. Then, she lost my favorite CD!

5. **shut down** (系統) 關閉；(工廠) 停工

  · That company shut down last week and many people were out of work.

Pop Quiz

Choose the answer that is closest in meaning with the underlined part.

(　　) 1. The operation of a large business needs a lot of effort and investment.

(A) malfunction　　(B) working　　(C) connection　　(D) equipment

(　　) 2. It was awful that we had a mishap with our car on the way to Kenting.

(A) accident　　(B) inspection　　(C) spot　　(D) defeat

(　　) 3. The bus service has connected all the towns with the big city.

(A) plagued　　(B) stranded　　(C) linked　　(D) conducted

(　　) 4. The students will make a visit to Taipei Zoo this Saturday.

(A) take place　　(B) call for　　(C) be known as　　(D) take a trip to

(　　) 5. To begin with, I didn't like Eva, but after I got to know her better, I found her a nice person.

(A) To sum up　　(B) In total　　(C) At first　　(D) At last

UNIT 18

Suicide Bombers Hit London

August, 2005

The city of London remains **on edge** after suffering suicide bombings, a failed bombing attempt, and the shooting of an innocent civilian.

The trouble began on July 7. In the city's worst suicide bombing attack ever, four suicide bombers **set off** bombs on London's public transportation system. Three explosions occurred on the city's subway system, also known as the Underground, and one bomb destroyed a double-decker bus. Altogether, 56 people were killed and hundreds more were injured in the attack.

Then, on July 21, London suffered yet another attack on its transit system. This time the bombs only partly detonated, and no one was killed. However, the entire city was shaken by this second attack, coming just two weeks after the first one.

The British Prime Minister, [1]Tony Blair, urged Londoners to stay calm and not to allow the attack to disrupt their normal way of life. Meanwhile, the police **stepped up** their hunt for potential suicide bombers and instituted a "shot-to-kill" policy. On July 22, one day after the second bombing, police officers shot and killed a suspected bomber in a London Underground station. It was later learned that the man, [2]Jean Charles de Menezes of [3]Brazil, was innocent and had no connection with any of the bombings.

Government officials apologized for the mistaken shooting but vowed to continue their efforts to prevent future bombings in the United Kingdom. Already, eleven people have been arrested in connection with the July 21 bombing. No arrests, however, have been made in the bombing investigation for July 7 attack. The police are still trying to determine if there is any connection between the two attacks.

Choose the best answers.

(   ) 1. Which of the following was not attacked in London in July, 2005?

(A) The transit system.　　　　　　(B) The Underground.

(C) The mass media.　　　　　　　(D) A double-decker bus.

(   ) 2. Which of the following statements about the police in the United Kingdom is NOT true?

(A) The police still try to prevent any future bombings in the UK.

(B) The police killed an innocent civilian after the July 21 bombing.

(C) The police have arrested eleven people related to the July 21 bombing.

(D) The police have proved that there is a connection between the two attacks.

(   ) 3. The phrase "**on edge**" in the first paragraph means that _____ .

(A) people in London will stay out of the city

(B) people in London are now peacefully safe

(C) people in London are very angry about the attacks

(D) people in London are nervous about the bombings

(   ) 4. Which of the following statements is true about the mistaken shooting?

(A) The civilian was shot because he came from Brazil.

(B) The British government has apologized for the mistaken shooting.

(C) The British government promised not to practice the "shot-to-kill" policy.

(D) Some of the government officials still thought that the civilian was guilty.

(   ) 5. Which of the following statements is true?

(A) Both of the two bombings have killed many Londoners.

(B) The Brazilian was shot right after the bomb detonated in July 21.

(C) Many Londoners decided to leave London after the second attack.

(D) The July 7 bombing has been London's worst suicide bombing attack ever.

1. **bomber** [ˋbɑmɚ] *n.* [C] 炸彈客

   bomb [bɑm] *vt.* 用炸彈攻擊；*n.* [C] 炸彈

   · Luckily, the suicide bomber was stopped before detonating the bomb.

   · The police have caught the man who tried to bomb the train station.

   · Don't get close to the bomb; it is very dangerous.

2. **shooting** [ˋʃutɪŋ] *n.* [C] 射殺，槍擊

   · The government is blamed for the mistaken shooting of the young man.

3. **innocent** [ˋɪnəsn̩t] *adj.* 清白的，無辜的

   · A person is always innocent before he or she is proved guilty.

4. **civilian** [səˋvɪljən] *n.* [C] 平民，百姓

   · Soldiers have to protect the civilians in their country.

5. **transportation** [͵trænspɚˋteʃən] *n.* [U] 運輸

   · The MRT is one of the public transportation systems in Taipei.

6. **Underground** [ˋʌndɚ͵graʊnd] *n.* [U] (the~) 地下鐵 (尤指倫敦地鐵)

   · Most of the Londoners go to work by taking the Underground.

7. **double-decker** [ˋdʌbl̩ ˋdɛkɚ] *n.* [C] 雙層巴士

   · I went to the British Museum by taking a double-decker in London.

8. **injure** [ˋɪndʒɚ] *vt.* 傷害

   · Be careful when you use the knife; you may injure yourself.

9. **detonate** [ˋdɛtə͵net] *vt.* 引爆

   · The criminal threatened to detonate the bomb if the police got any closer.

10. **prime minister** [ˋpraɪm ˋmɪnɪstɚ] *n.* [C] (the~) 首相

    · The British Prime Minister will make a speech on TV this afternoon.

11. **urge** [ɝdʒ] *vt.* 力勸，懇求

    · I urged my brother to do his homework instead of watching TV.

12. **potential** [pəˋtɛnʃəl] *adj.* 可能的，潛在的

    · Most of the young people are potential customers of the latest cell phones.

13. **institute** [ˋɪnstə͵tjut] *vt.* 制定

    · The government decided to institute new tax regulations.

14. **suspected** [səˋspɛktɪd] *adj.* 有嫌疑的

· The suspected murderer was caught and taken to the police station last night.

15. **apologize** [ə`pɑlə,dʒaɪz] *vi.* 道歉，認錯

· I apologized to Amy for forgetting to bring the book she wanted.

16. **vow** [vaʊ] *vt.* 發誓要做

· In the wedding ceremony, the groom vowed that he would love the bride forever.

17. **determine** [dɪ`tɝmɪn] *vt.* 查明，確定

· The police came to the building, trying to determine how it caught fire.

Idioms & Phrases

1. **on edge**　緊張不安

· Samantha was on edge before making her speech in the contest.

2. **set off**　引爆 (炸彈、爆竹等)

· It's illegal to set off fireworks in some states.

3. **step up**　加快

· The school officials are stepping up their efforts to reduce bullying at school.

Pop Quiz

Fill in each blank with the answer that matches the definition.

(A) injure	(B) urge	(C) suspected	(D) detonate
(E) vow	(F) potential	(G) Underground	(H) determine
(I) step up	(J) on edge		

_____ 1. to promise

_____ 2. considered to be guilty of a crime

_____ 3. to cause to explode

_____ 4. to increase the speed of a process

_____ 5. subway

UNIT 19

Tainted Products Spread Across the World

October, 2008

It first affected China, then spread to Taiwan and other parts of Asia, and is now causing problems in Europe and North America. Tainted milk and food products from China have raised fears around the world and caused many to question the safety of things they buy and eat.

The problems started in China earlier this year. There, it was discovered that some dairy farmers had added [1]melamine, an industrial chemical, to milk and milk powder. Melamine is primarily used in plastic manufacturing, but it can also be added to foods to increase their [2]nitrogen content, making them appear to be rich in protein. However, consuming too much melamine can lead to kidney stones, then to kidney failure, and eventually death.

This is exactly what happened in China. In September alone, more than 53,000 infants became sick after consuming baby formula powder that had been contaminated with melamine, according to government officials in China. Four of these children died. Understandably, this news caused panic in many parts of China, especially among parents who had given their children powdered baby formula. Children were rushed by terrified parents to local hospitals for check-ups.

In Taiwan, the news also caused concern. While Taiwan's [3]Department of Health has now **taken action** to **deal with** this issue, some have criticized the department—and the government—for being slow to react to this crisis. Fears were raised even higher after it was discovered that some creamers had also been tainted with melamine.

Although officials in China say that this problem is now under control, recent reports show a far different story. Contaminated candy has been found in Europe and the United States, and cookies and chocolates that were made in China are now also under investigation.

Yet, something positive might come out of this terrible crisis. Perhaps this food scare will lead to tighter regulations and stricter controls on food and dairy products in China. If so, people everywhere may once again start to feel secure about the things they consume, especially food products from China.

Choose the best answers.

(   ) 1. What might be a positive implication of the scandal of tainted Chinese dairy products?

(A) Sales of food exports from countries other than China will be increased.

(B) Stricter quality checks will be carried out on the Chinese dairy products.

(C) The public will go to hospital more often for medical check-ups.

(D) Food manufacturers will boost the protein content of their food products.

(   ) 2. Which of the following statements is NOT true?

(A) The Taiwanese government was fast to deal with the crisis.

(B) A low intake of melamine may not seriously damage one's kidneys.

(C) Melamine is an industrial material.

(D) The contaminated milk has made many infants become sick.

(   ) 3. Which of the following has happened since the scandal broke out?

(A) Children were sent to hospitals for medical examinations.

(B) The Chinese government managed to control the spread of the tainted milk.

(C) Investigation results proved all of the snacks from China to be harmful.

(D) People in China still bought the tainted dairy products.

(   ) 4. What can be inferred from this passage?

(A) Dairy farmers used melamine to make their products taste better.

(B) The Chinese government has been honest with the press.

(C) The safety of infants' food was seriously affected by this incident.

(D) Only China and Taiwan are affected by the tainted products.

(   ) 5. Health officials have conducted an investigation over foods _____ .

(A) to find out whether products are safe or meet quality standards

(B) to ensure that customers will remain loyal to the products

(C) so that countries around the world will place more orders for the products

(D) in case that hospitals will adopt the products as part of the diet for patients

1. **tainted** [`tentɪd] *adj.* 受污染的，受感染的
   · The tainted blood supply made people afraid of receiving blood transfusion.

2. **dairy** [`dɛrɪ] *n.* [U] 乳製品
   · Ken's father is a dairy farmer, and his family always have fresh milk at home.

3. **industrial** [ɪn`dʌstrɪəl] *adj.* 工業的
   · Industrial pollution has become a serious problem in developing countries.

4. **powder** [`paʊdɚ] *n.* [U] 粉末
   · You can make a cup of coffee by mixing the coffee powder with hot water.

5. **plastic** [`plæstɪk] *adj.* 塑膠的
   · Plastic bags are harmful to our environment, so we should use them less often.

6. **content** [kən`tɛnt] *n.* [U] 含量
   · The vitamin content of milk is rich.

7. **protein** [`protiɪn] *n.* [U] 蛋白質
   · Lack of protein can cause the loss of muscle mass.

8. **consume** [kən`sum] *vt.* 吃掉，喝掉
   · Mice have consumed all the food in the barn.

9. **kidney** [`kɪdnɪ] *n.* [C] 腎臟
   · Our kidneys can separate waste from our blood.

10. **infant** [`ɪnfənt] *n.* [C] 嬰兒
    · Infants need close physical contact and interaction with caring parents.

11. **formula** [`fɔrmjələ] *n.* [U] 嬰兒配方奶
    · When it comes to nutrition, formula can't replace breast milk.

12. **contaminate** [kən`tæmə,net] *vt.* 污染，毒害
    · The oil leak seriously contaminated the drinking water supply of this area.

13. **panic** [`pænɪk] *n.* [C] 驚恐，恐慌
    · The little girl got into a panic when she couldn't find her mother.

14. **terrify** [`tɛrə,faɪ] *vt.* 使害怕
    · The fierce storm terrified people in this village.

15. **check-up** [`tʃɛk ,ʌp] *n.* [C] 身體檢查
    · Mr. Lin has a check-up once a year to see if anything is wrong with his body.

16. **creamer** [`krimɚ] *n.* [U] 奶精
   - I don't like to add creamer to my coffee; I usually add milk instead.
17. **regulation** [ˌrɛɡjəˈleʃən] *n.* [C] 規定，規則
   - Not only drivers but also pedestrians should follow traffic regulations.
18. **secure** [sɪˈkjʊr] *adj.* 安全的
   - The baby girl felt secure in her mother's embrace.

Idioms & Phrases

1. **take action** 採取行動
   - We should take action to solve the pollution problem before it gets worse.
2. **deal with** 應付，處理
   - The government is having trouble dealing with drug problems.

Pop Quiz

Choose the best answer to each of the following sentences.

(　　) 1. If you want to lose some weight, you should stop ＿＿＿ fried chicken.
　　　　(A) consuming　　(B) terrifying　　(C) exploring　　(D) abusing

(　　) 2. We must avoid using too many ＿＿＿ bags because they are harmful to the environment.
　　　　(A) printed　　(B) primary　　(C) plastic　　(D) secure

(　　) 3. My family have regular dental ＿＿＿ every year.
　　　　(A) check-outs　　(B) check-ups　　(C) check-ins　　(D) check-offs

(　　) 4. The people in the store got into a(n) ＿＿＿ when the fire alarm went off.
　　　　(A) kidney　　(B) powder　　(C) infant　　(D) panic

(　　) 5. If the government doesn't ＿＿＿ right now, more people will lose their jobs.
　　　　(A) deal with　　(B) shut down　　(C) take action　　(D) turn in

UNIT 20

Taiwan Becoming an [1]M-Shaped Society

December, 2007

In the past, Taiwan's economy was the pride of Asia and the envy of the rest of the world. For many years, the economy in Taiwan was strong and it grew steadily. People around the island prospered and Taiwan's [2]middle class grew larger and larger. Recently, however, things have changed. Studies have shown that Taiwan's economy has now actually become more M-shaped, and it continues to move in this direction.

When an economy is M-shaped, there are a lot of people with low incomes and also a lot of people with high incomes. However, there aren't many people with average incomes. So, **basically speaking**, there are more rich people in Taiwan today than ever before. Yet, there are also more poor people in Taiwan now, and Taiwan's middle class is shrinking.

In addition, according to one government study, the average yearly income for the poorest households in Taiwan fell from 52,820 NT dollars in 2000 to 34,866 NT dollars in 2006. **On the other hand**, the average yearly income for Taiwan's wealthiest households grew from 1,621,747 NT dollars in 2000 to 1,741,669 NT dollars in 2006.

For those in the middle class, many have discovered that they are working longer hours, but are making less money than they did in the past. Some are under pressure to work overtime, but they do not receive any overtime pay or other benefits for putting in these extra hours at work. These people are sometimes known as the "working poor," and they often have jobs in sales, advertising, or the service industry. Sadly, the number of people who consider themselves as the "working poor" continues to grow.

So, it is clear that the economy in Taiwan is changing in many ways. Unfortunately, some of these changes are not good, since the gap between the very rich and the very poor in Taiwan continues to widen, and more and more people in the middle class are working longer hours for less money.

Choose the best answers.

(   ) 1. In an M-shaped economy, there are _____ .

    (A) not a lot of people with low incomes

    (B) not a lot of people with high incomes

    (C) not a lot of people with average incomes

    (D) a lot of people who are in the middle class

(   ) 2. Which of the following descriptions about Taiwan's economy is NOT true?

    (A) The average yearly income for the poorest family has fallen from the year 2000 to 2006.

    (B) The average yearly income for the wealthiest family has grown from the year 2000 to 2006.

    (C) The average yearly income for the middle class family has increased from the year 2000 to 2006.

    (D) People in the middle class find that they are working longer hours for less pay.

(   ) 3. Who do NOT belong to the "working poor"?

    (A) Salespersons.   (B) Waiters.

    (C) Waitresses.   (D) Teachers.

(   ) 4. How do the people in Taiwan's middle class feel about their jobs?

    (A) They think they are working longer hours for more pay.

    (B) They think they are working longer hours for less pay.

    (C) They think they are happy about working overtime because they receive some benefits.

    (D) They think if they work longer hours, they will be wealthier.

(   ) 5. How is the economy changing in Taiwan now?

    (A) The gap between the very rich and very poor widens.

    (B) More and more people are working longer hours for more money.

    (C) The number of the people who are in the middle class increases.

    (D) Taiwan's economy is not M-shaped anymore.

1. **economy** [ɪˋkɑnəmɪ] *n.* [C] 經濟結構，經濟制度
   · The weak economy has affected all the businesses in the country.

2. **envy** [ˋɛnvɪ] *n.* [U] 羨慕的目標
   · Germany has a good education system that is the envy of other countries.

3. **steadily** [ˋstɛdəlɪ] *adv.* 穩定地
   · Sales of organic food have been steadily increasing these years.

4. **prosper** [ˋprɑspɚ] *vi.* 繁榮
   · Switzerland has prospered and become one of the richest countries in the world.

5. **income** [ˋɪn͵kʌm] *n.* [C] 收入，所得
   · It is fair that people with high incomes pay higher rate of tax.

6. **average** [ˋævərɪdʒ] *adj.* 平均的
   · The average height of the players in this basketball team is 182 cm.

7. **shrink** [ʃrɪŋk] *vi.* 縮少，縮小 (～, shrank, shrunk)
   · Tina's property shrank because of a wrong investment in the stock market.

8. **yearly** [ˋjɪrlɪ] *adj.* 每年的，年度的
   · The yearly festival held by this small town always attracts lots of tourists.

9. **household** [ˋhaʊs͵hold] *n.* [C] 家庭，一家人
   · Joe was still studying after the other members of the household had gone to bed.

10. **wealthy** [ˋwɛlθɪ] *adj.* 富裕的
    · Janet comes from a very wealthy family. Her father is a rich businessman.

11. **pressure** [ˋprɛʃɚ] *n.* [U] 壓力
    · My brother put pressure on me not to tell Mom about his secret.

12. **overtime** [ˋovɚ͵taɪm] *adv.* 超時地；*adj.* 加班的；超時的
    · The machine broke down and the workers had to work overtime to fix it.
    · Buck worked extra hours in order to get more overtime pay.

13. **sales** [selz] *n.* (*pl.*) 銷售業；銷售額
    · Jeff is not only a successful businessman but an expert in sales and marketing.
    · Because of the depression, sales of cars are down this year.

14. **advertising** [ˋædvɚ͵taɪzɪŋ] *n.* [U] 廣告業
    · This food company spends 100 million dollars a year on advertising.

15. **service industry** [`sɝvɪs `ɪndəstrɪ] *n.* [U] 服務業

    · That "the customer is always right" is the first principle in the service industry.

16. **gap** [gæp] *n.* [C] 隔閡，差距

    · It needs a lot of effort to bridge the generation gap.

Idioms & Phrases

1. **basically speaking**   基本上來說

    · Basically speaking, your plan is good but not quite practical.

2. **on the other hand**   另一方面

    · On the one hand, they serve tasty food, but on the other hand, the service is slow.

Pop Quiz

Fill in each blank with the correct word to complete the sentence. Make changes if necessary.

average	prosper	wealthy	pressure
household	shrink	income	steady

1. Today, there are more and more _____ which have at least one TV set.
2. The fishing village has _____ since many tourists came to watch the whales nearby.
3. The doctor asked his patient to relax as much as possible and keep breathing _____ .
4. The _____ age of the engineers in this computer company is thirty-five.
5. Mr. Carlson is _____ and often donates much money to help those in need.

UNIT 21
Taiwanese Kids Drink More Soda than Water

October, 2007

Do you like to drink soda pop? Children in Taiwan definitely do. A recent study has revealed that 45 percent of children in Taiwan consume at least one soft drink every day. Many even drink more than one of these beverages **on a daily basis**.

The survey was conducted by a non-profit organization called the [1]Child Welfare League Foundation (CWLF). In total, more than one thousand fourth- and fifth-grade students around Taiwan were asked about their beverage-drinking habits.

A similar survey by the [2]World Health Organization showed that only children in [3]Israel drink more soda than children in Taiwan. Children in the United States and the United Kingdom, in comparison, drink less soda than kids in Taiwan, according to this survey.

The CWLF survey found even more surprising facts. Besides soda pop, many Taiwanese students admitted drinking sugary tea drinks, iced drinks, and even coffee every day. Shockingly, five percent of the students surveyed also said that they frequently bought alcoholic beverages.

In addition, the survey also showed that most children in Taiwan aren't drinking enough water. On average, students in Taiwan drink only 1,200 cubic centimeters (cc) of plain water every day, and ten percent drink just 500 cc of plain water each day. Both amounts **fall short of** the Taiwanese government's recommendation of 1,500 to 2,000 cc of water consumption each day.

If students want to **make sure** that they are drinking enough water, they should try to drink at least six glasses of plain water every day, according to the CWLF. Additionally, the CWLF says that parents can also play a role in getting their children to drink more water. Parents, for example, can **set a** good **example** for their children by drinking water, instead of soft drinks, themselves.

Reading Comprehension

Choose the best answers.

(　　) 1. How do we know from the passage that children in Taiwan like to drink soda pop?

(A) Children in Taiwan drink only 2,000 cc of water every day.

(B) Taiwanese children drink iced drinks, coffee and enough water every day.

(C) According to the survey by the World Health Organization, only children in Israel drink more soda than children in Taiwan.

(D) 5 percent of children in Taiwan drink at least one soft drink every day.

(　　) 2. Which of the following statements about the CWLF is true?

(A) The CWLF is a foundation which helps solve the problem of child workers in Asia.

(B) The CWLF found that children in Taiwan drink less soda than children in the United States.

(C) The CWLF recommends children to drink 1,500 to 2,000 cc of water each day.

(D) The CWLF suggests that parents set a good example for their children by drinking more water every day.

(　　) 3. How much water should children drink per day?

(A) At least six glasses of plain water.

(B) 1,200 cc of plain water.

(C) 500 cc of plain water.

(D) More than 2,000 cc of plain water.

(　　) 4. Which of the following statements about Taiwanese children is NOT true?

(A) Taiwanese children drink not only soda pop but also coffee and alcoholic beverages.

(B) Taiwanese children drink the most soda than any other countries in the world.

(C) The survey by the CWLF found that 45 percent of the fourth- and fifth-grade students in Taiwan drink at least one soft drink each day.

(D) On average, most of Taiwanese children drink 1,200 cc of water each day.

(　　) 5. What is the main idea of the passage?

(A) Parents in Taiwan drink more water than their children.

(B) The CWLF makes good contribution to the welfare of children in Taiwan.

(C) Drinking enough water every day can make people healthier.

(D) Children in Taiwan prefer drinking soft drinks to water.

Vocabulary

1. **soda pop** [`sodə ˌpɑp] *n.* [U] 汽水
   · Drinking too much soda pop is not healthy.

2. **beverage** [`bɛvərɪdʒ] *n.* [C] 飲料
   · Colored beverages usually contain chemicals which may do harm to your body.

3. **non-profit** [ˌnɑn`prɑfɪt] *adj.* 非營利的
   · The non-profit organization was set up to help people instead of making money.

4. **comparison** [kəm`pærəsn̩] *n.* [U] 比較
   · In comparison to Susan, Jenny is shy and quiet.

5. **shockingly** [`ʃɑkɪŋlɪ] *adv.* 令人震驚地
   · Shockingly, some of the best students cheated on the exam.

6. **alcoholic** [ˌælkə`hɔlɪk] *adj.* 含有酒精的
   · Don't drive after you consume alcoholic beverages. It's very dangerous.

7. **cubic centimeter (cc)** [`kjubɪk `sɛntəˌmitɚ] *n.* [C] 立方公分
   · Cubic centimeter is a unit for measuring space.

8. **plain** [plen] *adj.* 純的，不攙雜的
   · I never add sugar or creamer to my coffee. I like it plain.

9. **recommendation** [ˌrɛkəmɛn`deʃən] *n.* [C] 建議
   · Ann gave me a recommendation on a good book to read.

10. **consumption** [kən`sʌmpʃən] *n.* [U] 用量，消耗量
    · The consumption of oil has been increasing dramatically since cars were invented.

11. **additionally** [ə`dɪʃənlɪ] *adv.* 附加地，此外
    · We'll visit Japan next week. Additionally, we'll go to Bali after leaving Japan.

Idioms & Phrases

1. **on a...basis** 按…計算
   · All the rooms in the hotel are cleaned on a daily basis.

2. **fall short of** 低於預期的
   · The sales of laptops this year fell short of our expectations.

3. **make sure** 確定，確保
   · Make sure that all the doors and windows are locked before you leave the classroom.

4. **set a...example** 樹立…榜樣
   · Sophie is a diligent student and can set a good example for her classmates.

Pop Quiz

Fill in each blank with the correct word or phrase to complete the passage. Make changes if necessary.

recommendation	comparison	additionally	beverage
alcoholic	consumption	make sure	on a daily basis

Coffee has been used as a refreshing [1]_____ for more than a thousand years. However, nowadays there has been a controversy over the [2]_____ of coffee. Some specialists are making [3]_____ for frequent coffee intake to reduce the risk of diabetes because some chemicals in coffee help the body get rid of excess sugar. By contrast, other health professionals are warning that the caffeine in coffee can be a health hazard. This drug stimulates the kidneys, causing people to pass water more. [4]_____, coffee addicts may also become bad-tempered and moody between coffee "hits" during the day.

Although the findings seem contradictory, few scientists believe that moderate coffee drinking is harmful. Thus, for the good of health, it is advised that the intake of caffeine should be below 300 mg [5]_____.

UNIT 22

Terror Strikes [1]Mumbai

January, 2009

Terrorists attacked many different places in the heart of Mumbai, India in **a series of** coordinated strikes that began on November 26, 2008. Hundreds of people were killed or held hostage at several locations throughout the city. The siege ended 3 days later when commandos stormed the [2]Taj Mahal Palace and Tower Hotel and eliminated the last group of terrorists in a fierce battle.

Most of the violence occurred in the Taj hotel, a popular tourist destination. A total of ten terrorists also attacked several others places in Mumbai, including a [3]Jewish center and the largest train station in the city. The Indian government reported that 173 people were killed in shootings and bombings, and 308 people were wounded.

Officials stated that the attackers arrived by boat and quickly spread throughout Mumbai. The violence appeared to be random and the attackers did not target foreigners, as earlier reported. Police killed nine of the ten suspects during the fighting. The lone survivor, a 21-year-old [4]Pakistani man named Ajmal Amir Kasab, remains in police custody.

Questions instantly arose about the Indian government's ability to handle the terror attacks. Officials received warnings in 2007 that terrorists planned to hit Mumbai from the water, but the security forces did not have enough equipment and weapons to prevent such a large attack.

Evidence indicated that some Pakistan-based [5]Islamic groups may be responsible for the Mumbai attacks. After several weeks of the incident, the Pakistan government has arrested several members linked to the attacks. At the same time, Pakistan officials planned to work with India to take action to fight the terrorist activities.

Funerals and memorials have been held throughout India since the attacks, and Mumbai is struggling to regain its normal state.

Choose the best answers.

(   ) 1. When did the Mumbai terrorist attacks end?

(A) November 26, 2008.   (B) November 29, 2008

(C) November 23, 2008.   (D) It's not mentioned in the passage.

(   ) 2. Which of the following places was not attacked by the terrorists?

(A) A Jewish center.   (B) The Taj hotel.

(C) The largest train station in Mumbai.   (D) The Taj Mahal.

(   ) 3. Who was supposed to be the target of the Mumbai terrorist attacks?

(A) Foreigners traveling in Mumbai.

(B) No specific targets.

(C) The Indian government.

(D) A Pakistani man named Ajmal Amir Kasab.

(   ) 4. Which of the following statements is NOT true?

(A) 308 people were killed in the Mumbai terrorist attacks.

(B) The attackers entered Mumbai by sea and killed people at random.

(C) It is believed that some Islamic groups in Pakistan were behind the Mumbai attacks.

(D) The Mumbai terrorist attacks ended when the last group of terrorists was killed by the Indian soldiers in a hotel.

(   ) 5. How did the Indian and the Pakistan government respond to the terrorist attacks?

(A) The Indian government had received warnings earlier and was well-prepared for the terrorist attacks.

(B) The Pakistan government arrested a 21-year-old Pakistani man related to the attacks.

(C) The Indian government had enough weapons to prevent any attacks.

(D) The Pakistan government planned to work with India to fight against terrorists.

Vocabulary

1. **terror** [ˋtɛrɚ] *n.* [U] 恐怖

   terrorist [ˋtɛrəˌrɪst] *n.* [C] 恐怖份子

   · When the earthquake struck, many people ran out of their buildings in terror.

   · The car bombing last Friday carried out by terrorists killed at least ten people.

2. **coordinated** [koˋɔrdnˌetɪd] *adj.* 相互協調的

   · The task requires a coordinated approach to make the team work efficiently.

3. **hostage** [ˋhɑstɪdʒ] *n.* [C] 人質

   · Ten children on the school bus were taken hostage by two escaped prisoners.

4. **location** [loˋkeʃən] *n.* [C] 地點，場所

   · You can find the location of the airport on this map.

5. **siege** [sidʒ] *n.* [C] 圍困，包圍

   · Thousands of Thais have laid siege to the international airport for more than a month.

6. **commando** [kəˋmændo] *n.* [C] 突擊隊員

   · The Moscow police sent a 10-member team of commandos to solve the hostage crisis in the theater.

7. **eliminate** [ɪˋlɪməˌnet] *vt.* 根除

   · Some countries decided to take military action to eliminate Somalian pirates in the Indian Ocean.

8. **violence** [ˋvaɪələns] *n.* [U] 暴力

   · Children as well as teenagers should be protected from TV violence.

9. **destination** [ˌdɛstəˋneʃən] *n.* [C] 目的地

   · Bangkok is a popular destination among lots of European holidaymakers.

10. **wound** [wund] *vt.* 使受傷

    · The soldiers were seriously wounded in the terrorist attack.

11. **random** [ˋrændəm] *adj.* 隨機的

    · The lottery winning numbers are chosen in a random order by the computer.

12. **suspect** [ˋsʌspɛkt] *n.* [C] 嫌疑犯

    · The lady had been murdered at her apartment, and her husband was the suspect.

13. **survivor** [səˋvaɪvɚ] *n.* [C] 倖存者，生還者

    · Unfortunately, the rescue team saved only two survivors out of the collapsed building.

14. **custody** [ˋkʌstədɪ] *n.* [U] 拘留

　・ Five men who attacked the police in the protest were kept in custody for twelve hours.

15. **warning** [ˋwɔrnɪŋ] *n.* [C] 警告

　・ The weather report gives the public a warning about heavy rain tomorrow.

16. **security** [sɪˋkjʊrətɪ] *n.* [U] 安全

　・ For security reasons, all passenger baggage on the flight must be checked.

17. **evidence** [ˋɛvədəns] *n.* [U] 證據

　・ Evidence suggests that the suspect is linked to the murder of the famous billionaire.

18. **funeral** [ˋfjunərəl] *n.* [C] 喪禮

　・ Diana's funeral was held at Westminster Abbey, London on September 6, 1997.

19. **memorial** [məˋmorɪəl] *n.* [C] 紀念活動

　・ The government plans to hold a series of memorials to the victims of the atomic bombing.

Idioms & Phrases

a series of　一連串的…

　・ A series of rainy days ruined John's holiday plans.

Pop Quiz

Fill in each blank with the answer that matches the definition.

(A) hostage	(B) warning	(C) security	(D) random
(E) siege	(F) coordinated	(G) survivor	(H) eliminate

_____ 1. to kill someone in order to prevent them from causing trouble

_____ 2. a person who continues to live after an accident or illness, etc.

_____ 3. happening or chosen by chance

_____ 4. something that tells people to be careful before something bad or dangerous happens

_____ 5. safety from danger or loss

UNIT 23

The ¹NY Yankees' Taiwan Connection

June, 2005

It is a beautiful spring night at ²Yankee Stadium in New York City, and another sell-out crowd is ready to watch the New York Yankees play the ³Toronto Blue Jays.

But tonight is special. A closer look at the crowd reveals signs with the Chinese characters "jia you" and even flags from the Republic of China. And on the pitching mound is a tall pitcher from Taiwan. Wang Chien-ming, a twenty-five-year-old sensation, is making his ⁴Major League Baseball debut, and the world is watching.

Back in Taiwan, loyal fans, especially in Tainan, Wang Chien-ming's hometown, have high hopes for their hero. They believe that Wang, who was a star in Taiwan and who led Taiwan's baseball team to the Olympics in 2004, will be just as impressive in the "big leagues" of American professional baseball.

Fans in Taiwan and New York are not disappointed as Wang **puts in** a strong performance. He retires the first ten batters he faces and allows only six hits and two runs. Though Wang leaves the game in the seventh inning, the Yankees **go on** to win the game four to three.

Thus, Wang Chien-ming's historic debut as a New York Yankee has **come to an end**. Though Wang receives a start and not a win for the night, he does receive high praise for his performance. In fact, the Yankees' manager, Joe Torre, says that Wang is the best rookie pitcher he has seen in nine years.

Since his debut, Wang has compiled an impressive record of three wins and two losses. With such an impressive start to his rookie year, the future in Major League Baseball looks very bright indeed for Wang Chien-ming, the New York Yankee from Taiwan.

Choose the best answers.

(   ) 1. Where did Wang Chien-ming's debut game take place?

        (A) New York City.

        (B) Taiwan.

        (C) Tainan.

        (D) Toronto.

(   ) 2. Which of the following statements is true?

        (A) Wang Chien-ming is a player in the Toronto Blue Jays.

        (B) Wang Chien-ming led the American Olympic baseball team in 2004.

        (C) The New York Yankees' manager thinks Wang Chien-ming is the best rookie pitcher in nine years.

        (D) Wang Chien-ming has played in the Major League for more than twenty years.

(   ) 3. Wang Chien-ming _____ .

        (A) is a 24-year-old pitcher from Taiwan

        (B) made his Major League Baseball debut in Yankee Stadium

        (C) never played baseball in Taiwan

        (D) finished the whole game in his debut

(   ) 4. What is the result of Wang Chien-ming's debut game?

        (A) The Blue Jays beat the New York Yankees, 4 to 3.

        (B) The New York Yankees beat the Blue Jays, 5 to 4.

        (C) The Blue Jays beat the New York Yankees, 5 to 4.

        (D) The New York Yankees beat the Blue Jays, 4 to 3.

(   ) 5. Which of the following statements is NOT true?

        (A) Wang Chien-ming's hometown is Tainan.

        (B) Fans in New York and Taiwan are disappointed at Wang Chien-ming's performance.

        (C) Wang Chien-ming left the game in the 7th inning.

        (D) Wang Chien-ming retires the first ten batters.

Vocabulary

1. **connection** [kə`nɛkʃən] *n.* [C] 連接，關係
   · Willy's question didn't have the direct connection with our discussion.

2. **sell-out** [`sɛl͵aʊt] *n.* [C] *(sing.)* 滿座
   · The performance of Cloud Gate Dance Theatre of Taiwan was a sell-out tonight.

3. **character** [`kærɪktɚ] *n.* [C] 文字
   · Most Americans think that Chinese characters are difficult to write.

4. **pitch** [pɪtʃ] *vt.* (棒球) 投球

   pitcher [`pɪtʃɚ] *n.* [C] (棒球) 投手
   · The baseball player practices pitching for about three hours every day.
   · Wang Chien-ming is one of the pitchers in the New York Yankees.

5. **mound** [maʊnd] *n.* [C] (棒球) 投手丘
   · A mound is the place where a pitcher stands in a baseball game.

6. **sensation** [sɛn`seʃən] *n.* [C] 引起轟動的人或事物
   · Vincent's new novel is quite a literary sensation.

7. **loyal** [`lɔɪəl] *adj.* 忠貞的，忠實的
   · Soldiers should be loyal to their own country.

8. **impressive** [ɪm`prɛsɪv] *adj.* 給人深刻印象的
   · Mr. Richardson's speech was impressive and encouraging.

9. **professional** [prə`fɛʃənl] *adj.* 職業的；專業的
   · As a professional athlete, Tim always knows how to protect himself in a game.

10. **retire** [rɪ`taɪr] *vt.* (棒球) 使…出局；*vi.* 退休
    · The young pitcher surprised everyone by retiring Ichiro Suzuki (鈴木一朗).
    · Mr. Lin decided to retire after twenty-eight years' hard work.

11. **batter** [`bætɚ] *n.* [C] (棒球) 打擊者
    · Ichiro Suzuki is said to be the best batter in Asia.

12. **hit** [hɪt] *n.* [C] (棒球比賽的) 安打
    · The young batter's two three-base hits made himself the MVP today.

13. **run** [rʌn] *n.* [C] (棒球比賽的) 一分
    · The pitcher failed to stop the other team from having two runs.

14. **inning** [`ɪnɪŋ] *n.* [C] (棒球比賽的) 一局

· Our team finally had three runs in the second half of the ninth inning.

15. **praise** [prez] *n.* [U] 稱讚，讚美

· Anita's report has won her teacher's high praise.

16. **rookie** [`rʊkɪ] *n.* [C] 新選手，新球員

· The rookie hitter shocked everyone by hitting five home runs in one game.

17. **compile** [kəm`paɪl] *vt.* 編彙，收集 (資料)

· It took these scholars five years to compile the dictionary.

Idioms & Phrases

1. **put in** 投入 (勞／心力) 做…

· Victor Hugo put many years' work in writing his great piece, *Les Misérables*.

2. **go on** 繼續

· Jack was too tired to go on with his work, so he took a rest.

3. **come to an end** 結束

· The baseball game lasted for five hours and finally came to an end at 11:30 p.m.

Pop Quiz

Choose the answer that is closest in meaning with the underlined part.

(　　) 1. The newspaper is full of praise for Tom Hanks' performance in his new movie.

(A) appreciation　　(B) combination　　(C) definition　　(D) celebration

(　　) 2. Please write in bigger characters so that I can see them more clearly.

(A) performances　　(B) schedules　　(C) letters　　(D) responses

(　　) 3. It is believed that there is a connection between lung cancer and smoking.

(A) membership　　(B) relationship　　(C) determination　　(D) reaction

(　　) 4. The games between Yankees and Red Sox always attract lots of loyal baseball fans to the stadium.

(A) adorable　　(B) aggressive　　(C) generous　　(D) faithful

(　　) 5. The opera was so impressive that the audience clapped a lot when it finished.

(A) normal　　(B) unusual　　(C) sluggish　　(D) historic

UNIT 24

Tragedy Strikes Again at a US School

May, 2007

In the wake of the worst shooting massacre in modern American history, new details continue to **come out** about the killer and the events that happened that day.

On Monday, April 16, twenty-seven students and five teachers at [1]Virginia Tech were shot and killed by one gunman, [2]Cho Seung-hui. Cho, a 23-year-old English major at the university, eventually killed himself and brought the total number of people who died at the school that day to thirty-three.

Investigators say that the rampage began that morning when Cho entered a dormitory and killed a female student and a dorm supervisor. Then, Cho went to the post office to mail a package to [3]NBC News. A few hours later, Cho entered Norris Hall, chained the doors shut, and then walked from classroom to classroom, shooting students and teachers. Experts say that Cho fired more than 170 shots in nine minutes before shooting himself in the head.

Photos and videos from the package Cho mailed to the news station gave some information about Cho's motive for the killing spree. In the videos, Cho expressed his hate for the "rich kids" at Virginia Tech. He also praised the killers at [4]Columbine High School.

Yet, many people still wonder what could cause someone to commit such a terrible crime. Most people described Cho as a "loner," and family members said that Cho had always been a quiet child and rarely spoke in full sentences. As a result, he was often bullied at school. Cho had also been treated for mental illness while he was a student at Virginia Tech.

Perhaps the real reason for the killings will never be known. However, experts will continue to investigate this case in order to understand why it happened, in the hope of preventing another tragedy like this from ever happening again.

Choose the best answers.

(   ) 1. How many people did the gunman Cho Seung-hui kill except himself?

(A) 23.   (B) 32.   (C) 33.   (D) 27.

(   ) 2. The massacre at Virginia Tech started with _____ .

(A) Cho shooting students from classroom to classroom

(B) Cho mailing a package to the news station

(C) Cho killing a girl and a dorm supervisor

(D) Cho chaining the doors shut and committing suicide

(   ) 3. What might be the cause of Cho's killing spree?

(A) Cho hated himself for being too rich.

(B) Cho hated the rich kids in his school.

(C) Cho used to bully other students and thus felt guilty.

(D) Cho didn't make any friends and did poorly at school.

(   ) 4. Which of the following statements is NOT true?

(A) Cho was an active student leader and had held many activities at Virginia Tech.

(B) Cho suffered from mental illness when he was a student at Virginia Tech.

(C) Nobody knows exactly the reason why Cho committed such a terrible crime.

(D) Cho expressed his motive for the killing spree in the videos he made.

(   ) 5. The passage mainly talks about _____ .

(A) the way to prevent tragedies like the Virginia Tech massacre from happening

(B) the mental state of a student after being bullied

(C) how Cho fired more than 170 shots in nine minutes

(D) the worst shooting massacre in modern American history

1. **massacre** [ˈmæsəkɚ] *n.* [C] 大屠殺
   · Thousands of people got killed in the massacre during World War II.

2. **gunman** [ˈgʌnˌmæn] *n.* [C] 持槍歹徒
   · A gunman opened fire on the passersby and killed ten people.

3. **major** [ˈmedʒɚ] *n.* [C] 主修學生
   · My sister is a Japanese major in National Taiwan University.

4. **university** [ˌjunəˈvɝsətɪ] *n.* [C] 大學
   · Betty will study at a university in the United States after she graduates from senior high school next year.

5. **investigator** [ɪnˈvɛstəˌgetɚ] *n.* [C] 調查者；偵探
   · The investigator asked me if I saw anyone suspicious around before the robbery.

6. **rampage** [ˈræmpedʒ] *n.* [C] 狂暴的行為
   · The crazy man went on the rampage through the town and killed five people.

7. **dormitory** [ˈdɔrməˌtorɪ] *n.* [C] 學生宿舍 (簡稱 dorm)
   · Every student in this college lives in the dormitory.

8. **supervisor** [ˌsupɚˈvaɪzɚ] *n.* [C] 監督者；指導員
   · As a supervisor, Tony is in charge of almost everything in this department.

9. **chain** [tʃen] *vt.* 用鏈條拴住
   · Kevin chained up the dog in case it ran away.

10. **motive** [ˈmotɪv] *n.* [C] 動機
    · The motive of the mother who stole the bread is to feed her hungry kids.

11. **spree** [spri] *n.* [C] 無節制的從事某種行為
    · We went on a drinking spree in the pub and most of us finally got drunk.

12. **loner** [ˈlonɚ] *n.* [C] 孤僻的人
    · Mark is a so-called loner; he has no friends and likes to be alone.

13. **rarely** [ˈrɛrlɪ] *adv.* 很少，難得
    · I rarely eat fast food because I don't think it's good for my health.

14. **bully** [ˈbʊlɪ] *vt.* 恐嚇；欺凌
    · Poor Tommy was always bullied into giving away his pocket money.

15. **mental** [ˈmɛntl̩] *adj.* 心理的，精神的

· Too much pressure might cause mental or even physical problems.

16. **illness** [`ɪlnɪs] *n.* [C][U] 疾病

　　· Ivy suffered from a serious illness which made her take a semester off last year.

Idioms & Phrases

1. **in the wake of**　尾隨而至

　　· Tsunamis often follow in the wake of earthquakes in the sea.

2. **come out**　出現

　　· The news that the actress is dating a millionaire has come out.

Pop Quiz

Fill in each blank with the antonym (反義字).

| (A) physical | (B) motive | (C) chain | (D) bully | (E) loner |
| (F) cover up | (G) frequently | (H) major | (I) spree | (J) massacre |

_____ 1. rarely

_____ 2. set...free

_____ 3. mental

_____ 4. come out

_____ 5. party animal

UNIT 25

[1]World Cup Fever Sweeps the World

July, 2006

A special fever hit the world in June and July this year. Its "symptoms" included a keen interest in soccer, and people suffering from this "sickness" often **stayed up** late into the night to watch soccer matches. Some even cheered and danced in the streets, especially if their favorite player had scored a goal or their team had won. This special fever was, of course, World Cup fever. It strikes every four years, whenever the World Cup soccer tournament is being played.

This year, [2]Germany hosted the World Cup, and fans and supporters of the thirty-two teams in the tournament poured into the country. Even those without tickets still had fun as they watched the matches on big-screen TVs in public squares and cheered for their teams.

In Taiwan, World Cup fever was also very intense. Live World Cup matches usually began at 11 p.m. and some matches even started at 3 a.m.; however, bars and restaurants **were** still **packed with** cheering soccer fans at these late hours.

Gambling on the World Cup matches also reached a fever pitch as people all over the world bet on the outcome of the matches and on which team would win the tournament. The previous champion [3]Brazil was an early favorite, and many gamblers also bet on England. Therefore, when these teams lost, the people who had bet on these teams were often shocked and upset.

Although World Cup fever may have come to an end for this year, prepare yourself for 2010, when it will definitely strike again!

Choose the best answers.

(　　) 1. What is NOT one of the "symptoms" of the World Cup fever?

    (A) People would blame the coach for the loss of their favorite teams.

    (B) People would stay up late into the night to watch soccer matches.

    (C) People would pour into the country where the soccer tournament is held.

    (D) People would dance and cheer in the streets for their favorite players' victory.

(　　) 2. Which of the following statements about the soccer fans is true?

    (A) They fought with others when their teams lost.

    (B) They wouldn't watch the matches if they had no tickets.

    (C) They were too shy to cheer for their teams in the streets.

    (D) They watched the soccer matches on big-screen TVs in public squares.

(　　) 3. The author described the World Cup fever in a(n) _____ tone.

    (A) sad

    (B) angry

    (C) excited

    (D) nervous

(　　) 4. The word "**pitch**" in the fourth paragraph can be replaced by _____.

    (A) "the weakest part"

    (B) "the lowest place"

    (C) "the highest point"

    (D) "the loudest voice"

(　　) 5. What would make the soccer fans shocked and upset during the World Cup fever?

    (A) Tickets to the World Cup matches were sold out.

    (B) Watching the soccer matches in bars and restaurants.

    (C) Staying up too late into the night to watch soccer matches.

    (D) Losing the bets on the outcome of the soccer games.

Vocabulary

1. **fever** [ˈfivɚ] *n.* [C] *(sing.)* 狂熱
   · The terrifying movie "Ring" brought about a horror movie fever years ago.

2. **sweep** [swip] *vt.* 席捲，掃過
   · The typhoon swept the whole area and caused serious damage.

3. **symptom** [ˈsɪmptəm] *n.* [C] 症狀
   · Coughing is one of the symptoms of catching a cold.

4. **keen** [kin] *adj.* 強烈的，激烈的
   · James has a keen interest in playing online games.

5. **score** [skor] *vt.* 得分
   · Ken's shot scored two points in the last second and helped his team win the game.

6. **goal** [gol] *n.* [C] 球門；得分數
   · Paul scored two goals and became the MVP of the game.

7. **whenever** [hwɛnˈɛvɚ] *conj.* 每當⋯時
   · You can call me whenever you need help.

8. **tournament** [ˈtɝnəmənt] *n.* [C] 競賽
   · Teddy won the tennis tournament and we would celebrate tonight.

9. **host** [host] *vt.* 主辦
   · The United Kingdom will host the next Olympic Games in 2012.

10. **supporter** [səˈportɚ] *n.* [C] 支持者
    · Some soccer supporters began fighting after they knew their teams had lost.

11. **pour** [por] *vi.* 湧入，注入
    · Many tourists poured into Disneyland during the summer vacation.

12. **intense** [ɪnˈtɛns] *adj.* 強烈的
    · An intense feeling of disappointment struck Jim when he was rejected by Susan.

13. **gamble** [ˈgæmbl̩] *vi.* 賭博
    gambler [ˈgæmbl̩ɚ] *n.* [C] 賭徒
    · In Chinese New Year, we sometimes have fun by gambling on card games.
    · John is such a gambler that he spends all his money on horse racing.

14. **bet** [bɛt] *vi.* 打賭
    · I wouldn't bet on that baseball team if I were you.

15. **outcome** [`aʊtˌkʌm] *n.* [C] 結果
    · We were very disappointed at the outcome of the basketball game.
16. **previous** [`privɪəs] *adj.* 以前的
    · I have no previous experience in designing a website.
17. **champion** [`tʃæmpɪən] *n.* [C] 冠軍
    · The famous boxer was once the world heavyweight champion.

Idioms & Phrases

1. **stay up**　熬夜
    · Sandy stayed up late to study in order to pass the exam.
2. **be packed with...**　塞滿⋯
    · Taipei Zoo is always packed with adults as well as children on weekends.

Pop Quiz

Choose the best answer to each of the following sentences.

(　　) 1. Fever is usually considered as a _____ of illness.
      (A) tournament　　(B) symptom　　(C) system　　(D) champion

(　　) 2. Many people _____ into Time Square in New York City to welcome the New Year.
      (A) scored　　(B) reacted　　(C) poured　　(D) escaped

(　　) 3. _____ I see Jessica, she always wears a smile on her face.
      (A) Whichever　　(B) Whatever　　(C) Whoever　　(D) Whenever

(　　) 4. I was happy with the _____ of the football game—my favorite team won.
      (A) outcome　　(B) fever　　(C) goal　　(D) supporter

(　　) 5. With two children from her _____ marriage, Linda married her second husband.
      (A) intense　　(B) packed　　(C) previous　　(D) keen

NOTE

Translation
& Analysis

翻譯

2005 年 12 月

眾所皆知，美國人喧鬧而友善，法國人生性浪漫，日本人安靜多禮；但稍等一下，此等舉世普遍認同的刻板印象其實未必正確。近來有項新的研究顯示，雖然我們對於各國 (籍) 的人常有特定的刻板印象，但這些印象通常有違事實。

這項研究的結果發表於科學期刊上，研究過程中，4,000 位來自 49 種文化的人接受調查，指示他們描述一位自身文化中的代表人物，之後在另一項調查中，又被告知要描述自己以及出身相同文化的熟人。

兩項結果一經比對，結果卻有所出入，換言之，受訪者對於自身文化代表人物的看法，與他們對於自我的看法大不相同。

舉例來說，一般認為德國人做事條理分明且效率高，不過研究結果卻顯示，多數德國人完全不是這樣看待自己，他們可能覺得自己狂野、熱情、甚至是懶散。雖然他們明白有關德國人的刻板印象確實存在，甚至也相信其他德國人的行事風格的確如此，但他們卻認為自己是個例外。

從以上例子我們可以得知，刻板印象有多不可靠。因此，下回你打算用刻板印象來形容某人是「典型的」德國人，或是來自其他國家的「經典代表」人物時，請三思。該項研究中的一位研究人員說得或許最貼切：「各國人士的刻板印象或許可以提供某一文化的部分資訊，但卻不足以完整描述該國的人民。」

補充

1. **Science** 科學期刊

由美國科學促進會 (American Association for the Advancement of Science，簡稱 AAAS) 出版，內容主要刊登最新科學研究成果、與科學或科技政策相關新聞，以及各學科的原創論文等，是目前世界上最具權威性的學術雜誌之一。

解析

(C) 1. 本文第四段一開頭就提到：「舉例來說，一般認為德國人做事條理分明且效率高…」所以答案很明顯是 (C)。

（ A ）2. 本文第一段就點明對各國的刻板印象通常有違事實，因此答案為 (A)；第二段提到，受訪者必須描述一位自身文化，而非其他文化中的代表人物，因此 (B) 是錯的；第二段第一句中提到，這項研究的結果被發表於科學期刊上，因此 (C) 也是錯的；最後，在第二段中提到，接受訪問者是 4,000 位來自 49 種文化的人，但並未説明來自哪些國家，因此 (D) 也不能選。

（ D ）3. 本文第三段中提到：受訪者對於自身文化代表人物的看法，與他們對於自我的看法大不相同。所以答案為 (D)。

（ C ）4. 在最後一段中出現的 "unreliable" (不可靠的) 意思是 ＿＿＿＿＿＿＿。
(A) 不明確的　　　(B) 不重要的　　　(C) 不可靠的　　　(D) 可理解的

（ B ）5. 本文最後一段的結論中提到，「各國人士的刻板印象或許可以提供某一文化的部分資訊，但卻不足以完整描述該國的人民。」所以 (A) 不能選，因為刻板印象可用於瞭解文化，並非全然錯誤；(B) 是對的；(C) 是錯的，第四段提到，大多數的德國人行為舉止均與刻板印象不同，因此不能説是例外；(D) 是錯的，因為我們可以利用刻板印象來瞭解文化，但卻不能用它來瞭解個人。

Pop Quiz 解答

1. D　2. B　3. C　4. C　5. A

UNIT 02

翻 譯

2007 年 9 月

　　2007 年 8 月 20 日，驚傳中華航空編號 120 班機在日本爆炸，最終的下場悽慘又戲劇化。這架機型為波音 737-800 的客機當天從台北起飛，降落在沖繩縣的那霸機場，但當飛機正停妥在跑道上時，一具引擎開始冒煙並起火燃燒。

　　機場裡一位機警的地勤人員發現問題並通知機長，機組人員便立即開始為疏散機上所有人做準備，幸虧他們行動迅速，157 名乘客都得以在幾分鐘內離開。從戲劇化的影片鏡頭可以看到乘客從飛機的緊急逃生梯滑下，過了一會兒，這架華航的飛機便爆炸成一團巨大的火球，所幸機上所有的乘客和機組人員都安然無恙，只有少數幾個人受輕傷，無人在該事故中身亡或重傷。

　　日本的爆炸事件，對於華航在改善其名聲及飛安紀錄──曾被 CNN 形容為「全球飛安紀錄最糟的航空公司之一」──的努力，無疑是個重擊。事故發生前，專家認為華航已有改善並持續在進步，因為該公司上次的重大事故發生於 5 年前，但最近的這次爆炸卻再次引發人們對這家航空公司的關注與害怕。

　　調查人員已將恐怖行動排除於可能的爆炸原因之外，反之，他們表示最可能的原因是螺栓鬆脫、刺破飛機右翼的燃料箱，並造成油料的滲漏。有關爆炸原因以及華航機體維修方式的調查，目前則仍在持續進行中。

補 充

1. **China Airlines** 中華航空股份有限公司

    簡稱華航，成立於 1959 年，總公司位於台北市，是台灣最大的航空公司，其飛航路線包含亞洲、北美洲、歐洲以及大洋洲，此外也有國內航班。

2. **Boeing** [ˋboɪŋ] 波音公司

    世界知名的飛機製造商，總部位於美國芝加哥，該公司最為人熟知的機型即為波音 747。

3. **Okinawa** [ˌokɪˋnɑwə] 沖繩

    日本沖繩縣，大致範圍就是琉球群島，面積 2,273 平方公里，總人口約 136 萬，縣府為那霸市。

4. CNN (Cable News Network) 有線電視新聞網

美國最著名且最具影響力的有線電視新聞頻道，擁有多個有線電視及衛星頻道，據估計在全球有 15 億人口可以收看到 CNN 的節目。

解 析

(D) 1. 本文第一段第二句提到，該班機為波音 737–800 型飛機，因此 (A) 選項是錯的；第一段第一句說，該班機為中華航空編號 120 班機，因此 (B) 選項也是錯的；同樣在第一段第二句，文章提到該班機當天從台北出發，降落在沖繩縣的那霸機場，因此 (C) 選項是錯的；第二段第三句提到，機上全部 157 名乘客均離開了飛機，因此 (D) 選項為正確答案。

(B) 2. 文章第二段第三、四句提到，乘客在短短幾分鐘內全數撤離飛機，而在片刻後，飛機便爆炸起火，因此答案為 (B)。

(B) 3. 第三段中的 "turn the corner" (好轉；度過難關) 意思為何？
(A) 變換方向，改去其他地方
(B) 度過難關並開始改善
(C) 在空中盤旋後完美降落
(D) 藉由在空中多次轉彎來打破世界紀錄

(A) 4. 最後一段第二句中，調查人員表示，爆炸原因可能是鬆脫的螺栓刺破燃料箱所導致的油料滲漏，所以 (A) 是對的；第三段第二句句末提到，華航上一次的重大意外事故發生於 5 年前，所以 (B) 是錯的；本文只有在第三段的第一句中引述 CNN 的說法，且其內容是對華航的批評而非讚美，因此 (C) 是錯的；在最後一段的第一句中提到，調查人員已經排除了恐怖行動涉及這次事故的可能性，因此 (D) 選項也是錯的。

(C) 5. 本題考文章的主旨，從第一段說明華航空難的時間地點，第二段接敘發生經過，第三段說明空難在媒體及大眾間引發的效應，到最終段陳述可能的事發原因，通篇文章的主旨在說明這次的事件及其對華航帶來的負面影響。(A) 選項只涵蓋第二段內容；(B) 選項錯在該事件是發生於降落完成後，與飛行員技術無關；(C) 選項為正確答案；而由於整篇文章都沒有提到空服員，所以 (D) 選項很明顯也是錯的。

Pop Quiz 解答

1. D   2. G   3. A   4. E   5. H

翻　譯

2008 年 6 月

今年 5 月有 2 個亞洲國家分別遭到天災襲擊。第一個發生在緬甸聯邦，亦稱為緬甸。5 月初，強烈的熱帶氣旋猛烈襲擊該國，這個名為「納吉斯」的氣旋引發嚴重災害，造成數千人喪生，更多人無家可歸、無電可用或缺乏乾淨的水源。起初，緬甸行事隱密的軍政府不願公開當地災情的細節，並拒絕國際援助；然而，隨著損害程度的明朗化，該國政府終於軟化態度，慢慢開始接受來自其他國家的緊急物資。

接著，5 月 12 日下午 2 點 28 分，中國因強烈地震而天搖地動，該地震震度高達芮氏規模 7.9 級，是 30 餘年來中國所發生過最大的地震。位居中國西部的四川省，在這次天災中受創最重。這次地震的震央位在四川首都成都西北方約 80 公里的汶川縣，四川北部全區因建築物倒塌而喪生的就有數千人。

地震消息占據台灣新聞頭條版面，並在接下來幾天主導全球各地的新聞。許多新聞報導都將焦點放在地震中遭到摧毀的 6,898 間教室。總計有 6 萬 5 千人死於這場地震，36 萬人受傷，超過 2 萬 3 千人至今仍下落不明。

雖然四川地震受到媒體廣泛的報導以及舉世的關注，但緬甸的災情也同樣嚴重。報導指出，7 萬 8 千人死於此次氣旋，5 萬 6 千人仍行蹤不明，而有 100 萬人也因為這個氣旋無家可歸。此外，專家也擔心，由於救援耽擱再加上食物短缺，緬甸將可能有更多人喪命。

人在苦難時都需要援助，但遺憾的是，緬甸政府太晚接受其他國家提供的援助，再者，國際新聞媒體把焦點擺在中國，而非緬甸的災難，因此許多人都沒察覺到緬甸的情況有多嚴重。但有件事很清楚，就是近來緬甸和中國天災的受害者，目前比任何時候都更需要世人的關心與援助。

補　充

1. **Burma** [ˋbɝmə] 緬甸

緬甸聯邦的舊稱，自一九八九年緬甸軍政府更名後便不復出現於正式官方文件上，但在民間或非正式場合上仍有許多人使用。

2. **Nargis**　特強氣旋風暴納吉斯

全名 Very Severe Tropical Storm Nargis，是繼 2006 年的氣旋馬拉後第一個登陸緬甸的風暴，它橫掃緬甸南部海岸線，引起嚴重風暴潮，並造成極大破壞，導致至少 90,000 人死亡，56,000 人失蹤，是緬甸史上最嚴重的天災。

3. **Richter scale** [ˋrɪktɚ ˋskel] (the～) 芮氏地震規模

位於觀測點的地震儀會在地震發生時將震波記錄下來，芮氏地震規模便是利用震波最大振幅的常用對數演算而來，用於表示地震規模大小的標度。

解 析

(C) 1. 文章第三段第三句提到：總計有 6 萬 5 千人死於這次地震，因此選項 (A) 是對的；第四段第二句後半提到：有 5 萬 6 千人仍 (因氣旋) 行蹤不明，因此 (B) 也是對的；同樣在第四段第二句，「報導指出，有 7 萬 8 千人死於氣旋…」，而死於地震的如上文所提為 6 萬 5 千人，因此 (C) 是錯的，答案選 (C)；第三段最後一句提到，因地震而行蹤不明者有 2 萬 3 千人，而因氣旋而行蹤不行的人數為 5 萬 6 千人，因此 (D) 選項為真。

(C) 2. 從文章第一段中我們可以得知熱帶氣旋進犯的是緬甸，而第二段則指出四川省汶川縣遭強烈地震襲擊，所以 (A)、(B) 兩個選項是錯的；第二段第二句後半提到，這次襲擊四川的地震是三十餘年來，中國所發生過最嚴重的地震，因此 (C) 是對的；整篇文章描寫的都是在中國及緬甸所發生的天災，並未出現政府屠殺人民的敘述，因此 (D) 是錯的。

(B) 3. 從文章第二段第四句：「震央位在四川首都成都西北方約 80 公里的汶川縣…」中可知，四川首都為成都，因此 (A) 是錯的；震央位於汶川，因此 (B) 是對的；汶川位於成都的西北而非東南方，所以 (C) 是錯的；文章並未提及四川省最大的都市是哪一個，因此 (D) 無從判斷，不能選。

(A) 4. 從文章第四段一開頭：「…四川地震受到媒體廣泛的報導以及舉世的關注…」以及最後一段的第三句：「…國際新聞媒體把焦點擺在中國，而非緬甸的災難…」可知答案為 (A)。

(A) 5. 在文章最後一段的 "grave" (嚴重的，重大的) 意思為何？
(A) 嚴重的。　　(B) 感激的。　　(C) 容易的。　　(D) 生氣的。

Pop Quiz 解答

1. disasters　2. cyclones　3. As a result　4. devastation　5. In addition　6. victims

UNIT 04

不良行為與名人的錯誤示範

2007 年 1 月

過去幾個月來,台美兩地一些名人皆因不良行為而躍居頭條。在台灣,有七位藝人被檢測出使用非法藥物的陽性反應;而在美國,則是美國小姐因未成年飲酒而遭非議。

台灣方面,員警在台北一棟豪華公寓發現數百棵的大麻植株,以及內有多位知名藝人門號的手機一具。調查人員於是決定傳喚這些明星前來應訊。起初,這些明星一概否認曾經使用毒品,其中兩位電視綜藝節目主持人庹宗康和屈中恆甚至召開記者會,否認他們曾吸食大麻。然而,就在隔天,他們二人皆聲淚俱下地承認確實曾經使用非法藥物。

數週後,毛髮與尿液採樣證實,這些明星當中有七位確實曾使用過非法藥物,其中包含大麻和古柯鹼。雖然這些明星中的大部分都宣稱他們只在亞洲其他國家中使用這些毒品,但他們仍必須全體接受強制性的藥物勒戒療程。

另一場聲淚俱下的記者會則是在美國舉行。美國小姐塔拉・康娜承認她曾在紐約市的夜店中以未成年的身分飲酒。然而,在這位選美皇后與擁有環球小姐協會的知名億萬富豪唐納・川普見面後,川普決定給康娜一個自新的機會。在他們的記者會上,川普表示康娜是個「心腸不錯」的「好人」,她只是犯了些錯誤。她將被允許保留她美國小姐的頭銜,但仍必須進行勒戒療程並接受藥物測試。

許多人認為這些事件應該能為明星及公眾人物上一堂課。當明星犯了錯,他或她是可以選擇坦承錯誤或否認一切。不過,明星們應該明瞭,如果他們決定說謊,那麼等到真相被揭穿之後,一般大眾和粉絲對他們將自有評斷。此外,由於年輕人常模仿名人的行為,時下的名人對於自己的一舉一動應更加謹慎,且要勇於面對犯錯後的後果。

補 充

1. **Miss USA** 美國小姐

為環球小姐協會下的三項選美比賽之一,自 1952 年起每年都會舉辦一次。環球小姐協會下的另外兩項比賽為環球小姐 (Miss Universe) 以及美國妙齡小姐 (Miss Teen USA)。

2. **drug rehabilitation** 藥物勒戒

某種藥物或心理治療的統稱,其治療症狀為對某些物質的過度依賴,這些物質大都會對心理或精神造成顯著的不良影響,例如酒精、處方藥物或所謂的街頭毒品,像是古柯鹼、海洛因、安非他命等。

3. **Tara Conner** 塔拉・康娜

1985 年 12 月 18 日出生於美國德州達拉斯市，於 2006 年當選美國小姐，同年 12 月，爆發其未成年飲酒及吸食古柯鹼等醜聞，醜聞爆發後，主辦人唐納・川普決定保留其美國小姐的頭銜，但前提是她必須接受藥物勒戒。

4. **Donald Trump** 唐納・川普

1946 年 6 月 14 日出生於美國紐約市皇后區，是川普集團的行政總裁 (CEO)，主要經營房地產開發以及賭博娛樂場所，其總財產市值約為 29 億美金。出於個人興趣，川普自 1996 年起接手環球小姐協會，之後曾進行多項改革。

5. **Miss Universe Organization** 環球小姐協會

總部位於美國紐約市，由媒體集團 NBC 環球公司以及地產大亨唐納・川普所共同擁有，該協會擁有並負責主辦環球小姐、美國小姐以及美國妙齡小姐等三項選美比賽，目前主席為寶拉・舒嘉特 (Paula Shugart)。

解 析

(C) 1. 從文章第二段第四句：「…兩位電視綜藝節目主持人庹宗康和屈中恆甚至召開記者會，否認他們曾吸食大麻…」可知，他們召開記者會的目的在否認他們曾經吸食過大麻，因此答案為 (C)。

(A) 2. 從第二段第一、二句可以得知，警方是在一棟豪華公寓中找到大麻以及一支內有藝人門號的手機後，才決定要傳喚這些藝人，因此答案為 (A)。

(C) 3. (A)、(B)、(D) 三個選項在第四段最後一句：「她 (塔拉・康娜) 將被允許保留美國小姐的頭銜，但仍必須進行勒戒療程且接受藥物測試。」中都有提到，因此唯一「不會」的答案為 (C)。

(B) 4. (A)、(C)、(D) 三個選項的線索在最後一段的最後一句：「…年輕人常模仿名人的行為，時下的名人對於自己的一舉一動應更加謹慎，且要勇於面對犯錯後的後果…」中都可找到，因此答案為 (B)。

(A) 5. 最後一段中的片語 "serve as" (當成…) 可以用 ＿＿＿＿＿＿ 取代。
(A) 是 (be 動詞)　　(B) 挽救　　　　(C) 抄寫　　　　(D) 允許

Pop Quiz 解答

1. C　2. D　3. B　4. B　5. A

UNIT 05

翻 譯

2008 年 5 月

　　奧林匹克運動會期間本應充滿和平與善意，且傳統的盛事之一便是將奧運聖火從希臘傳送到賽會主辦國，然而今年在傳送過程中，卻一再遭到示威、抗議，甚至是衝突所打斷。

　　甚至連奧運聖火都還沒點燃，問題就出現了。2008 年初，西藏的僧侶、尼姑與西藏一般民眾就開始抗議，要為西藏部份地區爭取更多的自由，少數抗議人士甚至要求西藏獨立，並終止中國在當地的統治。在隨後的數週中，數人在動亂中喪命，其中藏人與漢人都有，雖然抗議未能成功地終止中國對西藏的佔領，但卻足以引起世人對當地情況的關注。

　　因此，奧運聖火在前往北京途中，行經歐洲幾個不同國家時，不僅遇到奧運的支持群眾，更有抗議人士。特別是在英、法兩國，奧運聖火的傳送在好幾個場合中都遭到示威群眾打斷，當中大多數是贊成西藏獨立的激進人士；在某些場合，抗議者只是高舉西藏旗幟阻撓，但在其他場合，他們甚至會試圖搶奪奧運火炬並加以熄滅。

　　距北京開幕儀式不到 100 天，奧運聖火目前已經抵達中國，我們可以斷言，聖火在那兒很可能會受到民眾的鼓舞歡迎，而非面對抗議者。然而，爭議仍然存在，因為中國官員表示，他們會繼續原本的計畫，將聖火送上聖母峰山頂，儘管有人批評此舉既欠缺考慮又充滿風險性。

　　8 月奧運場上是否有更進一步的抗議仍然不確定，但有件事可以肯定：2008 年的北京奧運之路到目前為止，可以說是困難重重。

補 充

1. **Olympics** [oˋlɪmpɪks] 奧林匹克運動會

　　由國際奧林匹克委員會主辦，始於 1896 年，是每 4 年一次的國際性運動會，其中包含多種體育運動項目，最早起源於古希臘，現在已是和平與友誼的象徵。

2. **Greece** [gris] 希臘共和國

　　簡稱希臘，位於歐洲東南部巴爾幹半島南端。北接保加利亞、馬其頓以及阿爾巴尼亞，東臨土耳其、瀕愛琴海，西南則有愛奧尼亞海以及地中海。希臘被譽為西方文明的發源地，歷史悠久，對三大洲的文化發展有重大影響。

3. **Tibetan** [trˋbɛtn̩] *adj.* 西藏的；*n.* [C] 西藏人

   Tibet [trˋbɛt] 西藏

   古稱吐蕃，位於青藏高原上，比鄰尼泊爾、不丹及印度等國，主要民族是藏人，語言為藏語，目前是中國統治下的一個自治區，首府位於拉薩。

4. **Beijing** [beˋdʒin] 北京

   中華人民共和國首都，是僅次於上海的中國第二大城。它擁有超過三千年的歷史，且由於有五個朝代曾定都於此，故文化古蹟眾多，同時它也是中國最大的陸空交通中樞、政治及文化中心，在 2008 年更成為夏季奧運的主辦城市。

5. **Mount Everest** [ˋmaunt ˋɛvərɪst] 聖母峰／珠穆朗瑪峰／艾佛勒斯峰

   位於中國和尼泊爾交界的喜馬拉雅山脈上，海拔 8844.43 公尺，終年積雪，是世界第一高峰。藏語的「珠穆朗瑪」意思是「大地之母」；西方稱此峰為艾佛勒斯峰，是紀念曾負責測量其高度的英屬印度測量局局長 George Everest。

解析

(A) 1. 本題線索在第一段第一句後半的文字 「…傳統的盛事之一便是將奧運聖火從希臘傳送到賽會主辦國…」，故答案為 (A)。

(B) 2. 從文章第一段最後一句、第三段第一、二句都可以明顯看出，本文所提到，阻撓聖火傳遞行程並引起混亂的，都是要為西藏爭取自由的抗議活動，因此答案為 (B)。

(D) 3. 從文章最後一段第一句「8 月奧運場上是否有更進一步的抗議仍然不確定…」中可以看出答案為 (D)。

(A) 4. 文章第四段的最後一句說：「…中國官員表示，他們會繼續原本的計劃，將聖火送上聖母峰山頂，儘管有人批評此舉欠缺考慮且充滿風險性…」，由此可知答案為 (A)。

(C) 5. 以下的哪一個字意思最接近第一段中的 "disrupt" (使中斷)？

   (A) 偶遇。　　　　(B) 慶祝。　　　　(C) 打斷。　　　　(D) 支持。

Pop Quiz 解答

1. B　2. C　3. C　4. A　5. D

UNIT 06

翻譯

2006 年 4 月

台灣正面臨近年來的一大難題──不是禽流感，也不是 SARS 捲土重來，而是信用卡卡債問題。

這問題好幾年前就已經存在，當時銀行開始推廣信用卡，而一般民眾辦卡也變得很容易。比方說，有些銀行提供各式各樣的免費辦卡禮來吸引人們的注意。其他銀行則推出免繳年費的信用卡。結果，銀行之間爭取更多顧客的競爭愈演愈烈，甚至開始有銀行開放讓學生及無固定職業的人辦卡。信用卡業務代表甚至在各購物中心和超市設立辦卡攤位，以增進人們申辦信用卡的便利性。同時，線上申辦也成為取得信用卡的另一條方便管道。

因此，現在有 900 萬的台灣人至少擁有一張信用卡，而其中大部分的人平均持有 4 至 5 張信用卡。而且，在台灣，有 260 萬持卡人尚有未付清的卡債。通常被稱為「卡奴」的這些人，欠下了龐大的債務，平均每人欠款 33 萬新台幣。很遺憾地，有些「卡奴」放棄了希望。警方表示，過去數月以來，每個月約有 40 人因信用卡問題自殺。

為了解決台灣的卡債問題，專家們認為銀行不該再讓民眾如此輕易地就能申請到信用卡，他們還說，台灣大眾也應被教導如何正確使用信用卡。此外，有些專家表示，政府官員應該修訂銀行法，如此一來，申辦信用卡的過程就能更為嚴謹並受到規範。

補充

1. **bird flu** [`bɝd `flu] 禽流感

   由病毒所引起的動物性傳染病，通常只會感染鳥類，自從 1997 年香港首次出現人類遭感染的病例後，便引起世界衛生組織的高度關注，2003 年禽流感曾在東亞爆發，造成多人喪生，之後更擴散到歐洲地區。

2. **SARS** 嚴重急性呼吸道症候群 (Severe Acute Respiratory Syndrome)

   非典型肺炎的一種，於 2003 年首次在越南發現，本病是由一種冠狀病毒所引起，傳染途徑則是近距離的飛沫傳染，根據世界衛生組織 (WHO) 的數據，本病致死率約為 7%～15%，但超過 65 歲的患者死亡率則高達 50% 以上。

3. **Banking Law** 銀行法

由政府制訂，用於規範金融機構業務活動之專門法律，內容大致是規定銀行有從事存款、放款、匯兌、投資業務等義務，以及銀行與客戶所發生之各種權利義務之對外司法關係等。

解　析

(C) 1. 從文章第三段第二、三句中可以看出，所謂卡奴，意思就是指尚有卡債尚未清償的人，因此答案為 (C)。

(B) 2. 第二段第四句指出，由於銀行同業間競爭激烈，導致部分銀行提供信用卡給學生以及沒有固定工作者，因此 (A) 是對的；第三段一開頭就指出，在台灣有 900 萬人至少有 1 張卡，而且其中的大部分平均擁有 4 到 5 張，因此 (B) 是錯的；第三段最後一句說：「…過去數月以來，每個月約有 40 人因信用卡問題自殺…」因此 (C) 是對的；第三段第二句指出，在台灣有 260 萬的持卡人有尚未清償的信用卡債，因此 (D) 也是對的。

(B) 3. 文章最後一段中提到，專家指出，要解決卡奴問題，需要銀行與政府雙方共同努力，因此 (A) 是對的；全文中並未提及討債公司，因此 (B) 是錯的；從文章第三段中可以看出，信用卡的氾濫導致許多民眾負債，甚至有人因此而自殺，明顯造成社會問題，因此可推斷 (C) 選項是對的；在文章最後一段，有關解決卡奴問題的對策中，作者表示銀行應該讓申請信用卡的過程更加嚴格，因此 (D) 也是對的。

(C) 4. 在第二段中的 "fierce" (激烈的) 意思是 ＿＿＿＿＿＿＿＿。
(A) 效率高的　　　　(B) 有爭議的　　　　(C) 強烈的　　　　(D) 感情的

(A) 5. 從文章第三段最後一句，我們可知 (A) 是對的；從文章最後一段中，我們可以推斷出，應對卡奴問題負責的除了銀行之外，還有制訂銀行法的政府，因此 (B) 是錯的；第三段中提到，台灣目前背負卡債者約有 260 萬人，平均每人負債 33 萬，卡債總額約為 8,580 億，所以 (C) 是錯的；從第三段可知，台灣約有 900 萬人持卡，其中 260 萬人背負卡債，不到一半，因此 (D) 是錯的。

Pop Quiz 解答

1. variety　2. fierce　3. at least　4. committed　5. meanwhile

《密碼》一片在爭議中開出好票房

翻 譯

2006 年 6 月

極具爭議性的新片《達文西密碼》正在全球戲院播放。該片肯定稱得上是賣座強檔，因目前進帳已超過 2 億 3 千萬美金。

本片根據暢銷的同名小說改編，由朗‧霍華執導，湯姆‧漢克斯主演，故事描述哈佛教授羅柏‧蘭登受法國警方之託，協助調查一起發生在巴黎羅浮宮的凶殺案。調查過程中，蘭登陸續發現各種象徵、密碼和線索，指引他揭露一個祕密團體與基督教間的驚人關係。

《達文西密碼》雖然票房得意，但許多影評卻大失所望。有的認為這部片流於普通，也有人認為十分無聊。甚至有影評直言，這部兩個半小時的影片過於冗長，因為片中演員一包括湯姆‧漢克斯在內一的演技都不夠搶眼。

此外，部分宗教團體也批評這部電影，認為內容對基督教徒十分冒犯，因為該片聲稱耶穌基督結婚且有後代，同時它也暗示天主教會多年來試圖掩蓋耶穌有後的「真相」。正因如此，梵蒂岡教廷譴責該片，希臘當地憤怒的基督教徒也要求禁播此片，而印度也有部分基督教徒甚至絕食抗議以抵制該片。

儘管部分保守的基督教徒及眾家影評大肆撻伐，世界各地的人仍持續湧入戲院欣賞《達文西密碼》。有的人是因為喜歡小說，有興趣觀看這故事的電影版，而一些人則是湯姆‧漢克斯的影迷，想一睹他的最新力作，還有更多人只是想親眼看看《達文西密碼》這部電影所引起的爭議到底是怎麼一回事。

補 充

1. **Ron Howard** 朗‧霍華

1954 年 3 月 1 日出生於美國奧克拉荷馬州鄧肯市，由於出身演藝家庭，自小就對電影事業深感興趣，1977 年首次執導，之後便陸續拍出多部叫好又叫座的電影，例如《浴火赤子情》(*Backdraft*, 1991)、《阿波羅 13》(*Apollo 13*, 1995)、《綁票通緝令》(*Ransom*, 1996) 等。

2. **Louvre Museum** [ˋluvrə mjuˋziəm] 羅浮宮

位於法國巴黎市中心塞納河畔，從前曾是法國國王的居所，現在則是收藏品多達 40 萬件的著名博物館，其收藏類別分為雕塑、繪畫、美術工藝、古東方、古埃及、古希臘、古羅馬等 7 項。

3. **Vatican** [ˋvætɪkən] 梵蒂岡

位於義大利首都羅馬市內西北角，是一個宗教領袖制國家，也是羅馬天主教會教廷所在地，語言為義大利語，以歐元為貨幣。雖然就面積而言，它是全世界佔地最小的國家，但在宗教及文化領域上，卻具有世界性的影響力。

解 析

(B) 1. 文章第一段第二句提到：「該片肯定稱得上是賣座強檔，因目前已進帳超過 2 億 3 千萬美金。」因此答案為 (B)。

(D) 2. 文章第三段最後一句中提到：「甚至有影評直言，這部兩個半小時的影片過於冗長，因為片中演員一包括湯姆・漢克斯一的演技都不夠搶眼。」因此答案為 (D)。

(C) 3. 在最後一段中的單字 "flock" (成群地去) 的意思為何？
   (A) 一群人一起上教堂。　　　　　(B) 一群人說同樣的話。
   (C) 一群人聚在一起做某件事情。　(D) 一群人一起對抗某件事物。

(B) 4. 文章第一段第二句便已經清楚說明它在票房上所創下的佳績，因此 (A) 是錯的；第二段第二句說明這部電影「描述哈佛教授羅柏・蘭登受法國警方之託，協助調查一起發生在巴黎羅浮宮的凶殺案。」因此可合理推測 (B) 是對的；第二段第一句提到這部電影是「根據暢銷的同名小說改編」，而非歷史事件，因此 (C) 是錯的；根據文章敘述，電影內容並不是達文西解開自己畫作的密碼，因此 (D) 是錯的。

(D) 5. 文章第四段中提到：「梵蒂岡教廷譴責該片」，且當地也有「憤怒的基督教徒要求禁播」，但並未提到教廷是否做出禁播與否的決定，因此 (A) 不能選；穆斯林指的是回教的信徒，而《達文西密碼》的內容主要是與基督教相關，因此 (B) 是錯的；第四段一開頭就提到：「部分宗教團體也批評這部電影，」因此 (C) 明顯也是錯的；(D) 是對的，從第四段第二、三句可以看出，電影中對於耶穌已婚生子，以及教會企圖掩飾這個「真相」的描述，正是引發爭議及批評之處。

Pop Quiz 解答

1. F　2. D　3. G　4. I　5. B

UNIT 08

翻 譯

2006 年 10 月

現今幾乎人手一台 MP3 隨身聽。特別是年輕人，經常可以見到他們一邊走路去上課、搭乘地鐵、或在健身房運動，一邊使用這些可隨身攜帶的音樂播放器聽著他們喜歡的歌曲。毋庸置疑地，MP3 隨身聽廣受歡迎，不過新的研究卻指出它們可能對我們的耳朵造成傷害。事實上，聽 MP3 隨身聽有可能影響一個人的聽力，最終甚至可能造成失聰。

英國最近一項調查發現，愈來愈多年輕人使用 MP3 隨身聽。該項調查中，有 14% 的人承認每星期使用 MP3 隨身聽的時數高達 28 小時；有些人甚至表示受到耳鳴之苦，這是聽力受損的明顯徵兆。然而，這些人表示，他們仍舊每天使用 MP3 隨身聽。

一位美國聽力學專家也針對 MP3 裝置的危險發出警告。如果噪音等級超出 85 分貝過久，人的聽力通常就會受損。糟糕的是，很多人聽 MP3 隨身聽的音量都超過 85 分貝，尤其是在運動健身的時候。這不僅對一個人的聽力有害，還可能對旁人造成危險，特別是當使用者在慢跑或是騎機車的情況下。

香港也有一位聽力專家針對很多人喜歡邊搭地鐵邊聽 MP3 隨身聽的習慣提出呼籲。由於在地鐵裡已經十分吵雜，聽 MP3 隨身聽的人一定得將播放器的音量調到更大才能聽清楚音樂。然而，此舉可能會造成聽力受損，甚至加速聽力喪失的發生。

因此，下次聽 MP3 隨身聽時不妨降低音量，或至少對可能的風險有所警覺。事實上，每當你使用耳機時，都應特別注意。其他人應該要聽不到你正在聽的音樂─如果他們聽得到，就代表音量過大。或者你可以選擇完全不用耳機聽音樂以保護你的耳朵。畢竟，聽力的損失是可以預防的。俗話說：「預防勝於治療。」所以，如果你現在使用 MP3 隨身聽的時候不多加注意，將來你可能聽不到你最喜歡的歌曲─或任何聲音。

補 充

1. MP3 player MP3 播放器

又稱為數位音訊播放器 (digital audio player，簡稱 DAP)，是一種可用於儲存、組織與播放音訊檔案格式的裝置，除了 MP3 (MPEG-1 Audio Layer 3) 檔案外，有些也可用於播放其它格式的檔案，例如 WMA、WAV 等。

2. **United Kingdom** [ðə juˋnaɪtɪd ˋkɪŋdəm] 英國 (the～)

即英國 (Britain)，其領土包含大不列顛島上的英格蘭、蘇格蘭、威爾斯，以及愛爾蘭島東北的北愛爾蘭，目前是世界上生活水準最高的國家之一。

解 析

(D) 1. 本題考文章主旨，首段指出聽 MP3 會對聽力有不好的影響，嚴重時甚至可能導致耳聾，第二段提到英國民調發現，常聽 MP3 的年輕人表示他們的聽力的確受到影響，三、四段則是美國及香港在聽力方面的專家警告：在嘈雜的環境中，人會將 MP3 音量調高，因而損害聽力，最後一段則建議聽 MP3 的人最好將耳機音量調小，或不用耳機，以保護自己的耳朵。從以上各段摘要可以看出，本文主旨在說明 MP3 會對聽力造成的傷害，以及該如何預防這類傷害，因此答案選 (D)。

(D) 2. 文章第二段最後兩句指出：有些人受到耳鳴之苦，但他們卻仍然每天使用 MP3 隨身聽，因此 (D) 是錯的。

(C) 3. 文章第三段指出，如果長時間處於 85 分貝以上的噪音環境中，人的聽力通常就會受損，而不幸的是，很多人常會將 MP3 的音量調到 85 分貝以上，尤其是當他們在運動的時候，因此答案選 (C)。

(A) 4. 以下哪一句諺語跟 "an ounce of prevention is worth a pound of cure" (預防勝於治療) 有相似的概念？
(A) 及時行事，事半功倍。　　　　(B) 風箏逆風，越挫越勇。
(C) 早起的鳥兒有蟲吃。　　　　　(D) 一張圖勝過千言萬語。

(B) 5. 文章第五段第三句中提到，使用耳機時，如果別人也聽得到音樂，那就表示音量太大了，因此 (D) 是錯的；下一句則說，為了保護耳朵，或許你應該選擇不用耳機聽音樂，因此 (A) 也是錯的；最後一句提到，如果使用 MP3 時不多加注意，以後可能沒辦法再聽自己最喜愛的歌，或任何聲音了，因此 (C) 是錯的，(B) 選項可在同段第一句後半找到，為正確答案。

Pop Quiz 解答

1. D　2. F　3. A　4. I　5. B　6. C

翻 譯

2006 年 2 月

多年來，光華商場一直是人們尋找及採購便宜電腦與電子用品的最佳去處。搜尋特價品的人不論老少，都定期到此採購電腦、電腦零組件與硬體設備、數位相機、MP3 播放器以及其他電子商品，他們往往將商場擠得水洩不通；舊書愛好者也常造訪光華商場，因為該處是北台灣二手書商的最大集散地。目前台北市政府已決定將商場關閉，將其搬遷至臨近的另一位址。

拆除光華陸橋的決定主要是基於安全考量。光華商場位居高架快速道路下方已逾 30 年，然而近年來，商場的安全問題愈趨嚴重，尤其是在經歷大地震後。因此政府決定將商場遷移至一處臨時地點，同時，一棟永久性的新商場大樓也正在新生南路上建造。

光華商場於 1973 年春天開幕，原本是為二手零售書商所設。之後，玉器和古董商人也開始在此營業。到了八〇年代，台灣的電腦與電子製造業開始蓬勃發展，商場零售商也開始銷售電子零組件與電子設備。由於商家之間的激烈競爭導致物品售價維持低廉，光華商場的人氣也越來越高。

光華商場的永久新址預計於 2007 年 2 月完工，但是一些台北居民表示，他們仍會懷念那擁擠繁忙的老商場，以及他們在那裡討價還價的種種回憶。

補 充

1. Guanghua Market 光華商場

原本位於台北市中正區光華陸橋下方，是舊書攤商與電腦資訊業者結合而成的綜合商場，2006 年 1 月光華陸橋拆除後，暫時遷往附近搭蓋的臨時屋中，直至 2008 年 7 月，位於新生北路與市民大道路口，名為「光華數位新天地」的大樓完工，才與西寧南路電子廣場的商家共同進駐，成為今日的光華商場。

解 析

(C) 1. 文章第三段第一句提到：「… 1973 年春天開幕…」，因此答案為 (C)。

(D) 2. 文章一開頭就提到：光華商場一直以來都是「人們尋找及採購便宜電腦與電子用品的最佳去處」，因此答案為 (D)。

（ D ）3. 第二段中提到，光華商場「位於高架橋下已經超過 30 年」，明顯老舊，再加上受「地震」影響，結構極不穩定，因此「基於安全考量，」決定拆除光華橋，而商場位於橋下，也勢必要因此而搬遷，因此答案選 (D)。

（ C ）4. 文章第三段最後一句提到光華商場之所以聲名大噪，就是因為「商家之間的激烈競爭導致物品售價維持低廉，」因此答案為 (C)。

（ C ）5. 從第二段第三句中的「商場的安全問題愈趨嚴重」，可以得知 (A) 是對的；最末段第二句中提到，台北市民「仍會懷念那擁擠繁忙的老商場」，因此 (B) 是對的；文章第一段就點明，光華商場是「北台灣二手書商的最大集散地」，因此 (D) 正確；(C) 是唯一錯誤選項，因為讀完全文，就可以知道在光華商場販賣的商品有電腦、二手書、玉器和古董，但並不包含衣服。

Pop Quiz 解答

1. C　2. D　3. B　4. A　5. B

影星希斯‧萊傑於 28 歲隕落

2008 年 2 月

　　1 月下旬，世人痛失一位前途看好的新生代演員。1 月 22 日，《斷背山》影星希斯‧萊傑被發現於紐約市過世，但目前仍不知他確切的死因。

　　目前已知的是，萊傑在其公寓臥室中被發現時，全身赤裸、面部朝下趴在床邊，在一旁還找到處方安眠藥。

　　起初，萊傑之死被報導為自殺，然而部分醫學專家現在卻改口，說他的死亡可能是個意外。他們表示，萊傑可能不小心混用了處方藥物。在他的住宅中並未發現任何不法藥物。

　　萊傑因為演出《決戰時刻》、《騎士風雲錄》等電影而開始踏上星途，之後在李安的賣座電影《斷背山》中飾演同性戀牛仔而廣受好評。萊傑也因為在該片中的演出，獲得奧斯卡獎提名。獲知萊傑辭世後，李安表示和萊傑共事是「我生命中最純真的喜樂之一」。

　　令人惋惜的是，萊傑在其演藝事業如日中天時殞落。他剛完成《蝙蝠俠：黑暗騎士》的拍攝，在這部即將上映的電影中，他擔綱演出「小丑」的角色。先前的報導提到，這很可能是他從影以來最細膩的演出。不過萊傑表示，這個角色讓他感到相當吃力，在他過世前幾週的一次訪談中，萊傑評述：「上個禮拜我可能每晚平均只睡 2 個小時，我的思緒停不下來，身體雖然疲憊，但腦袋卻一直在運轉。」

　　萊傑身後留有妻子和一名幼女，在澳洲當地家人的要求之下，他的遺體已被運回祖國，並將安葬在他的故鄉伯斯近郊。

1. Heath Ledger 　希斯‧萊傑 (1979-2008)

　　澳洲籍電影明星，2008 年 1 月 22 日被發現死於其紐約市的寓所，死後於 2009 年獲得奧斯卡金像獎的最佳男配角獎項。

2. Brokeback Mountain 　斷背山

　　改編自 Annie Proulx 的短篇小說，由台灣導演李安在 2005 年拍攝成電影，內容主要描寫深刻的同性戀情誼。

3. The Patriot 　決戰時刻

2000 年的電影，由 Roland Emmerich 執導，描述 18 世紀美國獨立戰爭的英雄事蹟。

4. **A Knight's Tale**　騎士風雲錄

2001 年的電影，由 Brian Helgeland 執導，描述 13 世紀歐洲的騎士故事。

5. **Ang Lee**　李安 (1954–)

台灣出身的電影導演，曾因「斷背山」獲得奧斯卡金像獎最佳導演獎項。

6. **Oscar**　奧斯卡金像獎

正式名稱為 Academy Awards，由「美國電影藝術與科學學院」所頒發，鼓勵優秀電影創作與發展的獎項，被視為全球電影界的最高榮譽。

7. **Perth** [pɝθ] 伯斯

澳洲西部的最大城市，人口約為 150 萬。

解 析

(D) 1. 從文章第一段第三句 "The exact cause of his death, however, still remains unknown at this time." 中，我們可以得知，希斯‧萊傑的確切死因仍不得而知，因此答案為 (D)。

(A) 2. 希斯‧萊傑被發現時，陳屍於紐約市自家公寓的臥室中，線索在第一段第二句 "found dead in New York City" 以及第二段第一句 "discovered in the bedroom of his apartment"，第二段第二句說明當時他全身赤裸 "naked"、面部朝下、趴在床邊 "lying face-down beside his bed"，從以上說明可以得知，除了選項 (A) 以外，其他都是錯的。

(A) 3. 第五段提到，希斯‧萊傑死時正處於他演藝事業的高峰，當時他剛結束在《蝙蝠俠：黑暗騎士》中的拍攝，在該影片中他飾演反派小丑，而這個角色被視為是他從影以來最細膩的演出，因此答案為 (A)。

(B) 4. 文章最後一段中的單字 "survive" 意思是「活得比…長」，答案選 (B)。

(A) 5. 由文章最後一段第二句：「在他澳洲當地家人的要求下…」可知，希斯‧萊傑出生於澳洲，因此答案選 (A)。

Pop Quiz 解答

1. A　2. C　3. B　4. D　5. C

翻 譯

2007 年 2 月

2007 年一開始，台灣人民見證了本島最新最快的鐵路開始營運——台灣高速鐵路 (THSR)。今年 1 月開始，以時速 300 公里行駛的列車，在台灣兩個最大都市——台北、高雄之間往返，載運旅客。這趟路程搭乘舊式火車需費時 4 至 6 個小時，但現在藉由搭乘新式的高速列車，已縮短成 90 分鐘。

許多人希望新式的高速鐵路服務能為台灣帶來好處，尤其是生活在本島西部，也就是高鐵行經區域的數百萬民眾。一位研究人員預測：「隨著高鐵通車，台灣島將成為台灣市。」根據一些專家的看法，台灣高鐵降低了交通的時間和成本，並增進台灣城市之間的聯絡，這些將使「台灣市」得以在經濟上與亞洲其他領先城市，例如香港和上海來競爭。

然而高鐵計畫自宣布以來也是爭議不斷。部分人士抨擊高鐵從原本選定的歐規轉變成日本的「子彈列車」技術；另外也有人在路線建造期間，引用報告指出了財務、安全及結構上的問題。而台灣高鐵的通車日期從原定的 2003 年，因種種原因而數度延後；近來票務問題更讓許多旅客不悅，對於高鐵車位預訂和購票的不便大失所望。

台灣高鐵是否真能改變台灣人生活、工作、旅遊的風貌呢？目前要斷定還言之過早，不過以其 150 億美元的造價，台灣人民都希望對國家而言，高鐵是一項值回票價的投資。

補 充

1. **Taiwan High Speed Rail** 台灣高速鐵路

簡稱台灣高鐵，於 2007 年初通車，其車體技術採用日本的新幹線系統，軌道則採用歐洲系統，其連結點包含西部各縣市及台北、高雄、台中等三大都會區，全長 345 公里，時速可高達 300 公里以上，從台北到高雄只需 90 分鐘。

2. **Hong Kong** 香港

全名為香港特別行政區，位於珠江口以東、華南沿岸，由香港島、九龍半島、新界以及 262 個島嶼所組成，清朝戰敗後遭英國殖民，直至 1997 年 7 月，香港主權才交還中華人民共和國，但在外交及軍事外仍享有高度自治權。

3. bullet train　子彈列車

將「磁性懸浮」原理應用在鐵路運輸系統上，使列車得以完全脫離鐵軌而懸浮行駛，由於完全沒有摩擦阻力，因此速度大幅提昇。一般子彈列車的時速大約在 300 公里左右。行駛於日本新幹線的列車也屬於子彈列車的一種。

解析

(C) 1. 根據文章第二段最後一句，高鐵之所以能讓台灣與亞洲其他領先城市競爭，是因為它 "decreasing travel time and costs"(降低了交通的時間和成本)，同時也 "increasing communications between Taiwan's cities"(增進台灣城市之間的聯絡)，因此答案選 (C)。

(C) 2. 文章第三段最後一句中提到，"ticketing problems have upset many customers"(票務問題讓許多旅客不悅)，而其中又包括訂位 (reserving seats) 問題以及購票 (buying tickets) 問題，因此答案選 (C)。

(D) 3. 本題問主旨，因此需整合各段重點方能答題：一、二段説明高鐵完工，使得台灣各城市間往返的時間縮短、成本降低，並讓台灣得以與其他亞洲城市競爭，第三段談高鐵所引起的爭議以及所受到的批評，末段結論則説高鐵可能對台灣人民帶來的影響尚無定論，但期盼它是一項對國家有利的投資。從以上重點可知，本文主旨在討論高鐵的影響，答案選 (D)。

(D) 4. 本題問高鐵相關問題，選項 (A) 錯在高鐵原本預計於 2003 年，而非 2007 年開幕 (第三段第四句)；(B) 錯在票務及訂位系統讓許多旅客不悅，而非沒問題 (第三段第五句)；(C) 錯在高鐵速度是每小時 300 公里，而非每分鐘；(D) 高鐵花費 150 億美元建造，為正確答案 (第四段第三句)。

(C) 5. 本題選何者有誤，選項 (C) 錯在並非所有台灣人都對高鐵系統滿意。文章第三段指出，它在系統從歐規轉為日規時曾遭到批評；施工期間，它在財務、安全、結構上的問題，以及它工程上的延宕等等都曾引發民眾不滿；而正式啟用後，在票務及訂位系統使用上的不便更為人所詬病。

Pop Quiz 解答

1. technology　2. communication　3. debuted　4. controversial　5. upset

UNIT 12

駭人雙颶風重創路易斯安那州紐奧良

翻　譯

2005 年 10 月

對許多美國人來說，今年 9 月是個可怕的月分，過去數週以來，接連兩個強大的颶風重創美國墨西哥灣沿岸地區，特別是紐奧良。颶風不僅導致數百人喪生、數千人無家可歸，更造成超過一千億美元的損失。

這場災難始於 8 月 29 日的卡崔娜颶風，起初災情似乎沒那麼慘重，但之後數日，多處潰堤使紐奧良幾乎完全泡在水裡，某些地方水深更達 20 呎 (6 公尺)，全市停電並缺乏乾淨水源多日。由於淹水情形十分嚴重，卡崔娜颶風遠離後數日，許多居民仍受困家中，有些人甚至爬上屋頂以躲避高漲的洪水，並等候救援。專家表示，此次颶風引發的洪水，其實比颶風本身更具破壞性。

整體而言，卡崔娜颶風共造成一千八百多人死亡，以及超過一千億美元的損失，是美國史上損失最為慘重的天災。雖然多數政府官員同心協力援救災區民眾，但許多人仍垢病中央政府應變遲緩。

不幸的是，卡崔娜颶風離開後，災難還沒結束，另一個五級的麗塔颶風於 9 月 21 日侵襲災區，造成紐奧良部分地區再度被洪水淹沒。

紐奧良和墨西哥灣沿岸居民都希望今年颶風季節的最壞狀況已經結束，許多人目前已重返家園，開始踏上重建破碎生活的艱困過程。

補　充

1. **New Orleans** [njuˋɔrliəns] 紐奧良

   美國路易斯安那州第一大城，同時也是歷史悠久的古城，原屬法國，但在 1803 年與路易斯安那州一併售予美國，19 世紀期間港口貿易繁榮，許多歐洲人湧入，帶來豐富的移民文化；2005 年 8 月則因卡崔娜颶風來襲而遭受重創。

2. **Hurricane Katrina** 卡崔娜颶風

   2005 年 8 月 29 日以每小時 233 公里的中心風速登陸美國路易斯安那州，造成紐奧良百萬人撤離、至少 1,833 人死亡、30 萬以上兒童無家可歸、財產損失超過 1,250 億美金，是大西洋颶風有史以來損失最為慘重的一次風災。

3. Hurricane Rita　麗塔颶風

2005 年 9 月 24 日凌晨以每小時 190 公里的中心風速登陸美國德州與路易斯安那州之間的海岸地區，登陸時伴隨著 3 公尺高的風暴潮，其強度甚至一度超越卡崔娜，總計造成 130 萬居民撤離、7 人死亡，財產損失約為 10 億美金。

解析

(C) 1. 從文章第一段最後一句以及第二段第五句可以看出，這兩次颶風帶來了「數以百計的人喪生、數千人無家可歸」(hundreds dead and thousands homeless)、「數十億美元的損失」(billions of dollars in damage) 以及紐奧良「停電並缺乏乾淨水源多日」(left without clean water or electricity for several days)，因此 (A)、(B)、(D) 三個選項是正確的；全文均未提到金價上漲 (the rise of gold price)，因此 (C) 是錯的。

(A) 2. 文章第二段第三句提到 "several levees broke"，下一句緊接著說 "New Orleans was almost completely flooded" (紐奧良幾乎完全泡在水裡)，因此可推測出 "levees" 應該是用於防水的堤防，答案選 (A)。

(A) 3. 本題選錯誤敘述，第一個選項 (A) 就錯了，從文章第二段第三句中可以看出，卡崔娜颶風過後水患嚴重，造成多處堤防被沖毀；麗塔颶風是在卡崔娜颶風之後才來襲，當時已經沒有什麼完整堤防留存下來了。

(B) 4. 文章第三段最後一句提到，美國中央政府因為其 "sluggish" 的反應而遭受大眾批評，由此可推測其意思應該是「遲鈍的；遲緩的」，答案選 (B)。

(D) 5. 本題選正確敘述，(A) 是錯的，因為從第二段第三句開始的敘述可知，為紐奧良帶來巨大災害的並非卡崔娜颶風本身，而是颶風過後的嚴重水患；(B) 也是錯的，第二段倒數第二句提到有些人會 "climbed to their rooftops to escape the rising waters and await rescue"，所以爬上屋頂是等待救援，而非救助他人；(C) 是錯的，美國政府遭到批評是因為其反應遲緩，而非破壞堤防；從第二段最後一句可以得知，比起颶風本身，颶風所帶來的水患危害更大，因此 (D) 為正確答案。

Pop Quiz 解答

1. C　2. C　3. A　4. D　5. B

UNIT 13
2005年奧斯卡金像獎《登峰造擊》擊退《神鬼玩家》

2005 年 3 月

　　雖然今年的奧斯卡頒獎典禮換了新的主持人，但卻少有驚喜，預期的熱門影片最終都贏得奧斯卡獎項。

　　晚會最大贏家是《登峰造擊》，這部描述一位女性拳擊手的電影，不僅勇奪最佳影片獎，更為克林‧伊斯威特贏得最佳導演獎；該片中飾演拳擊手的希拉蕊‧史旺也奪得奧斯卡最佳女主角獎，這是她繼 2000 年之後，第二度奪下影后寶座；而在片中飾演年長退休拳手的摩根‧費里曼，則獲得最佳男配角獎。

　　《神鬼玩家》表現不如預期，這部大成本的影片敘述特立獨行的億萬富豪—霍華‧休斯的故事，由知名演員李奧納多‧迪卡皮歐領銜主演。雖然這部影片獲得奧斯卡 11 項提名，但卻只贏得 5 個獎項，其中包括最佳女配角獎的凱特‧布蘭琪。最令人失望的可能是《神鬼玩家》未能拿下最佳影片和最佳導演獎，這也是該片導演馬丁‧史柯西斯第 5 度在奧斯卡抱憾。

　　前脫口秀諧星傑米‧福克斯以他在《雷之心靈傳奇》中飾演歌手雷‧查爾斯的表現，榮獲最佳男主角獎。在其得獎致詞中，他特別感謝已故祖母在他成長過程中的指引。

　　總計全美約有 7,000 萬人全程或花部分時間收看今年的奧斯卡頒獎典禮。

1. Clint Eastwood　克林‧伊斯威特

美國導演，1930 年 5 月 31 日出生於加州舊金山，自 1955 年起進軍演藝圈，曾擔任演員、電影導演與電影製片，其執導的電影超過 25 部，首次獲得奧斯卡金像獎最佳導演獎是在 1992 年，當時執導的電影是《殺無赦》(Unforgiven)。

2. Hilary Swank　希拉蕊‧史旺

美國女演員，1974 年 7 月 30 日出生於內布拉斯加州的林肯城，曾經兩度獲得奧斯卡金像獎最佳女主角獎，得獎電影分別是 1998 年的《男孩別哭》(Boys Don't Cry) 以及 2004 年的《登峰造擊》(Million Dollar Baby)。

3. Howard Hushes　霍華‧休斯

美國富豪，1905 年 12 月 24 日出生於德克薩斯州休斯頓，1976 年 4 月 5 日逝世，享年 70 歲。他不但是當時世上最富有的人之一，也是航空家、工程師、企業家以及電影導演，其傳奇性的一生曾於 1977 及 2004 年被改編為電影。

4. **Martin Scorsese**　馬丁‧史柯西斯

美國導演，1942 年 11 月 17 日出生於紐約市，1974 年首度執導，曾於 2007 年以《神鬼無間》(*The Departed*) 一片獲得奧斯卡金像獎最佳導演獎。

5. **Jamie Foxx**　傑米‧福克斯

非裔美籍男演員，1967 年 12 月 13 日出生於德州泰瑞爾，2004 年以《雷之心靈傳奇》獲得奧斯卡金像獎最佳男主角獎；他同時也是一位節奏藍調歌手，曾在 2006 年獲葛萊美獎節奏藍調及饒舌樂類 4 項提名，可惜均未獲獎。

6. **Ray Charles**　雷‧查爾斯

1930 年 9 月 23 日出生於美國喬治亞州奧爾巴尼，他是歌手、鋼琴家、編曲家，也是節奏藍調的開創者，曾列名於《滾石雜誌》「100 位最偉大藝人」之一，亦是法蘭克‧辛納屈眼中「音樂界唯一的天才」，2004 年 6 月 10 日逝世。

解　析

(B) 1. 本題問為何今年 (2005) 的奧斯卡沒有太多的驚喜，答案在第一段："as most of the predicted favorites ended up winning Oscars"，答案選 (B)。

(C) 2. 本題問是誰贏得最佳導演獎，答案在第二段第二句："This film...the best director award for Clint Eastwood"，答案選 (C)。

(D) 3. 本題問有關 Jamie Foxx 的敘述何者有誤，答案為 (D)，線索在第四段第二句："Foxx thanked his deceased grandmother for..." 既然他的祖母已故，當然不可能在現場看他領獎。

(C) 4. 本題問《神鬼玩家》在今年的奧斯卡表現不佳是因為：(A) 錯，因為得到最佳導演獎的是《登峰造擊》的導演克林‧伊斯威特 (第二段第二句)；(B) 錯，因為李奧納多在該片中是飾演男主角 (第三段第二句)，不可能入圍最佳男配角；(D) 錯在這是部大成本電影，因此失敗絕非因為預算不足 (第三段第二句)；因此答案為 (C)(第三段第三句)。

(D) 5. 本題問《登峰造擊》的內容是為何，答案為 (D)，線索在第二段第一、二句："... *Million Dollar Baby*. This film about a female boxer..."

Pop Quiz 解答

1. B　2. D　3. C　4. C　5. A

UNIT 14

「母親」──最美麗的英文字

翻 譯

2005 年 1 月

你最喜歡的英文字有哪些？你認為最美麗的英文字又是哪一個呢？在世界各地推廣英國文化及英語學習的英國文化協會，決定要找出英語當中最受歡迎以及最為人鍾愛的英文字。因此，該協會進行了一項調查，在 102 個非英語系國家中，詢問了 4 萬人，請他們講出最喜歡的英文字。

英國文化協會最近公佈結果，列出全世界最受喜愛的 70 個英文字，根據這項調查，「母親」是最受歡迎的一個，而有趣的是，「父親」這個字卻榜上無名。全球人士喜愛的字還包括「熱情」、「微笑」、「愛」與「永恆」。一位英國文化協會的官員認為，名列前茅的都是有力而正面的字。

榜上也有幾匹黑馬，名列其中的一些冷僻字包括「躲貓貓」、「目瞪口呆的」、「袋鼠」和「喂」；另外，「意外驚喜」、「文藝復興」、「多話的」等文學字眼也頗受歡迎；當然，有幾個俚語用字，像是「哎喲」和「很棒的」也獲選。

調查結果也顯示，某些英文字的人氣竟然可以在極短時間內竄升，像是榜上排名第 59 的「搖擺不定」是直到最近幾年才被廣泛使用。這個字在 2004 年美國總統大選期間大受歡迎，當時共和黨人士指責民主黨總統候選人約翰·凱瑞在許多議題上「搖擺不定」，立場不斷改變。

英國文化協會是為了慶祝該協會的 70 週年紀念才做了這次的問卷調查。

補 充

1. **British Council** [ðə `brɪtɪʃ `kaʊnsl̩] 英國文化協會 (the～)

   1934 年於英國成立之國際組織，目的在促進英國文化、教育與國際關係之拓展與交流，在全球 109 個國家中設有分部，提供英語教學、留學情報以及免費諮詢等多項服務，其在台分部成立於 1996 年，台北及高雄均有其據點。

2. **Republican** [rɪ`pʌblɪkən] *adj.* 共和黨的；*n.* 共和黨員

   Republican Party 為美國兩大政黨之一，創立於 1854 年，當時主要成員為部分民主黨人士及奴隸解放運動者，其主張為美國現代化，及反對奴隸制度的擴張。現今共和黨主張社會保守主義與經濟自由主義，前任美國總統喬治·布希便是共和黨員。

3. **Democratic** [ˌdɛməˋkrætɪk] *adj.* 民主黨的

Democratic Party 為美國兩大政黨之一，創立於 1792 年，以自由主義為主要政策，他們支持民權運動，直至 1993 年比爾·柯林頓時期才逐漸轉為中間派立場，目的在吸引共和黨選民。2008 年 11 月 4 日當選的美國首位非裔總統歐巴馬便是民主黨員。

4. **John Kerry** 約翰·凱瑞

1943 年 12 月 11 日出生於科羅拉多州奧羅拉，為美國民主黨員，同時也是代表麻薩諸塞州的參議員，2004 年曾獲民主黨提名，與共和黨候選人喬治·布希競選第 43 任美國總統一職，但最後並未當選。

解 析

(C) 1. 第一段第四句說明該調查以 "40,000 people in 102 non-English speaking countries" 為詢問對象；而第二段第二句則表明，根據調查，" 'mother' is the most popular word in the English language"，因此答案選 (C)。

(B) 2. 本題問哪一項敘述有誤，從三段第二句可知，"peekaboo," "flabbergasted," "kangaroo," 以及 "oi" 都是 "unusual words that made the list"(榜上有名的冷僻字)，可知 "oi" 並非 "popular and common words"，答案選 (B)。

(A) 3. 本題問 "loquacious" 屬於哪一類字，答案在第三段第三句："Literary words, such as... and 'loquacious'"，所以選 (A)。

(C) 4. 本題問英國文化協會並未做過的事，答案選 (C)「拒絕將調查結果出版」，線索在第二段第一句："...the British Council has published the results...English words."

(D) 5. 有關 "flip-flop" 一字的線索，可在文章第四段中找到：(A) 是錯的，因為 "flip-flop" 是 "the fifty-ninth most popular word"，而非 "forty-ninth"；(B) 是錯的，因為它的意思是 "change one's position on many issues"，剛好與 (B) 選項所說的意思相反；(C) 也是錯的，它第一次出現是被用於指責民主黨總統候選人，並非如選項所說的是被民主黨總統候選人所用，故答案選 (D)。

Pop Quiz 解答

1. D　2. A　3. D　4. B　5. C

UNIT 15

翻 譯

2008 年 12 月

　　今年秋天，巴拉克・歐巴馬獲選第 44 任美國總統，美國歷史新頁於焉展開。他是第一位取得此一職位的非裔美國人。在 11 月 5 日的這場重要選舉中，眾多美國人現身投票，讓民主黨黨員歐巴馬得以擊敗共和黨的約翰・麥肯。

　　巴拉克・歐巴馬 在 1961 年 8 月 4 日出生於夏威夷，父親是來自肯亞的黑人，母親則是堪薩斯州的白人。他的父母在幾年後離異，接著歐巴馬的母親再婚並舉家搬往印尼，歐巴馬在當地的公立學校就讀至 10 歲，之後又由母親帶他回到夏威夷。從哥倫比亞大學畢業後幾年，歐巴馬決定搬到芝加哥，擔任當地的社區組織工作者，接著，在投身政治之前，他還去念了哈佛大學的法學院。

　　身為伊利諾州資淺參議員的歐巴馬，在他 2004 年於民主黨全國大會發表演說前一直默默無名。這場演說名為「無畏的希望」，它震撼了群眾的心，也讓歐巴馬一夕之間成為全國家喻戶曉的人物。儘管如此，3 年後當他做出競選總統的選擇時，仍讓許多人感到訝異，因為在當時，希拉蕊似乎是民主黨候選人的不二人選。歐巴馬先是在初選中勝過希拉蕊，接著又在今年 11 月的大選中擊敗麥肯。

　　歐巴馬的勝選一經宣布，不僅在全美，在世界各地也同樣引爆慶祝風潮，在哈林區、肯亞、甚至日本的小濱市 (同樣叫做 Obama)，民眾都奔上街道載歌載舞。而在芝加哥，有超過 30 萬人聚在一起，聆聽歐巴馬發表演說。在慶祝歷史性的這一刻，並聆聽歐巴馬演說的同時，許多人，其中包括電視名人歐普拉・溫芙蕾與人權領袖傑西・傑克森在內，都不禁潸然淚下。

　　在演說中，歐巴馬嚴肅地提到美國正面臨的挑戰，他稱之為「我們人生中最大的 (挑戰)—兩地的戰爭、處於危險的星球、以及百年來最嚴重的金融危機」。然而，如同歐巴馬在競選過程中就曾做過的，他帶給美國人與全世界「希望」與「改變」，正如歐巴馬當晚所說：「就在這場選舉中，就在這決定性的時刻，『改變』已降臨美國。」

補 充

1. Obama　歐巴馬

　　巴拉克・歐巴馬 (Barack Obama)，美國第 44 任總統，在 2008 年 11 月 5 日代表民主黨在總統大選中獲勝，並於 2009 年 1 月 23 日宣誓就職，為美國第一位黑人總統。在此之前，他從 2004 年至 2008 年 11 月擔任伊利諾州的聯邦參議員。

2. **John McCain** 約翰‧麥肯

美國政治人物，曾於 2008 年代表共和黨參選美國總統失利。現為亞利桑那州聯邦參議員。

3. **Kenya** [ˋkɛnjə] 肯亞共和國

位於非洲東部，原為英國殖民地，於 1963 年 12 月 12 日獨立。面積約 58 萬平方公里，人口 3800 萬。肯亞的經濟活動以農業、旅遊業為主。

4. **Kansas** [ˋkænzəs] 堪薩斯州

美國中部的一個州，位於美國本土的正中心，是相當重要的農業州，首府位於托皮卡 (Topeka)。

5. **Indonesia** [ˏɪndoˋniʒə] 印度尼西亞共和國

簡稱印尼，位於東南亞；由上萬個島嶼組成，為全世界最大的群島國家，橫跨亞洲及大洋洲。印尼面積約 192 萬平方公里，人口 2 億 3700 多萬，是世界上人口第 4 多的國家，僅次於中國、印度和美國。

6. **Columbia University** 哥倫比亞大學

世界最具聲望的高等學府之一，位於美國紐約市。

7. **Harvard Law School** 哈佛大學法學院

哈佛大學是一所位於美國麻薩諸塞州波士頓近郊的私立大學，是美國歷史最悠久的高等學府。哈佛大學的法學院頗負盛名，在全美排名第二。

8. **Illinois** [ˏɪləˋnɔɪ] 伊利諾州

位於美國中北部，密西根湖的西南方，最大城市是芝加哥，首府位於春田市 (Springfield)。

9. **Hillary Clinton** 希拉蕊‧柯林頓

現任美國紐約州聯邦參議員，美國第 42 屆總統比爾‧柯林頓之妻。希拉蕊在 2008 年民主黨總統初選中敗給歐巴馬，但在歐巴馬當選總統之後，已經同意出任下屆國務卿。

10. **Harlem** [ˋhɑrləm] 哈林區

哈林區是美國紐約市曼哈頓的一個區域，曾經長期是 20 世紀美國黑人文化與商業中心，也是犯罪與貧困的地區，目前正在經歷一場社會和經濟復興。

11. **Oprah Winfrey** 歐普拉‧溫芙蕾

女性黑人，美國著名脫口秀節目主持人。

12. **Jesse Jackson** 傑西‧傑克森

美國黑人民權運動牧師，在 1980 年代曾經參選美國總統大選。

解析

(B) 1. 本題問為何本文標題為「歐巴馬締造歷史」，答案在第一段第一、二句："History was made in America...when Barack Obama was elected the forty-fourth president... Obama is the first African-American ever to hold this position."，亦即歐巴馬是美國歷史上首位當選總統的非裔美籍人士，答案選 (B)。

(B) 2. 本題問有關歐巴馬的敘述何者有誤？ 答案選 (B)，線索在第二段第三句："Obama's mother then remarried and moved the family to Indonesia, where Obama went to a public school until he turned ten." 由本句可知，歐巴馬 10 前是在印尼的公立學校就讀，而非夏威夷。

(B) 3. 本題問在 2007 年之前，誰是民主黨角逐次年總統寶座最可能的候選人？答案在第三段第三句後半："...since Hillary Clinton seemed the likely Democratic candidate at that time"，答案選 (B)。

(D) 4. 本題問有關歐巴馬勝選後的相關慶祝，何者敘述為真？(A) 是錯的，因為名為 Obama 的城市是在日本，而非肯亞，線索在第四段第一句；(B) 也是錯的，同樣在第四段第一句可以找到：慶祝活動橫跨全美，並非只侷限在芝加哥；(C) 是錯的，第四段第二句提到，歐巴馬勝選後的演說，地點是在芝加哥，而非夏威夷；答案選 (D)，在第四段最後一句中可以看到，包含主持人歐普拉以及民權運動領袖傑西在內的許多人，都為這歷史性的一刻而感動落淚。

(A) 5. 根據本文，我們可以推測：(B) 是錯的，第五段第一句，歐巴馬在其演講中所提到，我們目前必須面對最大的困難之一，便是 "the worst financial crisis in a century"；(C) 是錯的，第四段第一句中提到，當宣佈歐巴馬勝選時，哈林區與肯亞的民眾特別興奮，甚至上街載歌載舞的慶祝，那是因為他們與歐巴馬同為非裔人士，由此可推斷，住在哈林區的應該大多是黑人；(D) 是錯的，從第二段敘述可知，歐巴馬曾住過夏威夷、印尼、芝加哥，但從未在日本定居過，因此答案為 (A)，文章第四段最後一句提到，Jesse Jackson 為人權領袖，由此可推斷，他應該是為非裔美籍人士人權而奮戰的人。

Pop Quiz 解答

1. B　2. A　3. C　4. C　5. D

UNIT 16

音樂祭延期，不減搖滾感力

翻 譯

2006 年 8 月

　　國際海洋音樂祭今年再度撼動全台。今年的音樂祭一連 3 天在台北縣貢寮鄉的福隆海水浴場舉行。原本預定在 7 月 14 日周末所舉行的音樂祭，因熱帶風暴碧利斯而被迫延期；所幸接下來的週末天氣好轉，音樂祭也在凱米颱風影響活動之前順利畫下句點。

　　多年以來，國際海洋音樂祭一直扮演著一個重要角色，那就是將新音樂和新表演團體介紹給台灣樂壇。今年音樂祭的特色是，受邀前來的 54 個樂團在 2 個不同舞台上演出。活動最後一天的週日還有場樂團大戰，許多人都將這當成是音樂祭的重頭戲。去年的海洋音樂祭大賞得主「圖騰樂團」今年也在表演之列，其他著名的樂團還包括中國的搖滾團體「黑豹」以及「唐朝」。

　　然而，整個活動也並非全無爭議。今年海洋音樂祭的新主辦單位為民視，有些樂迷和音樂人便抱怨這個新主辦單位讓音樂祭太過商業化；另外，交通也是一團混亂。活動結束後，從福隆回到台北的路程，有人竟然就花了 6 個多小時。

　　儘管有這些問題，2006 年的國際海洋音樂祭依舊人氣十足，數千人共同度過了一個美好的週末，他們在沙灘上放鬆享受，聆聽超棒的現場音樂。樂迷們都希望明年的音樂祭能像今年一樣撼動台灣，也希望下一屆的國際海洋音樂祭不會再度因為天候不佳而被迫延期了！

補 充

1. **Hohaiyan Rock Festival**　　國際海洋音樂祭

　　一年一度的夏日音樂表演活動，首次舉辦是在 2000 年，由於地點均位於台北縣貢寮鄉境內的福隆海水浴場，因此又被稱為貢寮海洋音樂祭。**Hohaiyan** 為原住民語言，是與海浪有關的語氣詞。

2. **Fulong**　　福隆

　　即台北縣貢寮鄉福隆村，舊名為新澳底，觀光景點包含福隆海水浴場、隆隆山登山古道、草嶺隧道以及靈鷲山無生道場等，名產為福隆便當。

3. **Tropical Storm Bilis**　　熱帶風暴碧利斯

　　2006 年 7 月 13 日於宜蘭縣頭城鎮附近登陸的熱帶氣旋，雖然其強度尚未到達颱風的程度，但帶來的暴雨仍造成台灣農業超過 1 億元新台幣的損失。

4. **Typhoon Kaemi**　凱米颱風

2006 年 7 月 24 日晚間於台東縣成功鎮登陸的輕度颱風，隔天出海，並減弱為強烈熱帶風暴，在台期間帶來豪雨，所幸並未釀成重大災害。

5. **Totem** [`totəm] 圖騰樂團

成立於 2003 年 3 月，團員以台灣原住民為主，包含主唱兼吉他手 Suming、主唱查瑪克、吉他手阿新、鼓手阿勝以及唯一的漢人貝斯手 Awei，其音樂融合原住民吟唱、嘻哈、搖滾等不同風格，曾於 2005 年獲得貢寮海洋音樂祭大賞。

6. **Black Panther** [ˌblæk `pænθɚ] 黑豹樂團

成立於 1987 年的中國搖滾樂團，目前成員包括主要創作人兼吉他手李彤、主唱秦勇、貝斯手王文傑、鼓手趙明義以及鍵盤手馮小波，該樂團被視為是近代中國原創搖滾樂的先驅，知名歌曲包括 Don't Break My Heart、無地自容等。

7. **Tang Dynasty** [ˌtæŋ `daɪnəstɪ] 唐朝樂團

成立於 1988 年，是中國第一支重金屬風格的搖滾樂團，團員包含主唱兼吉他手丁武、吉他手陳磊、吉他手劉義軍、貝斯手顧忠以及鼓手趙年，知名歌曲包括夢回唐朝、飛翔鳥、太陽等。

8. **Formosa TV**　民間全民電視公司

簡稱民視，成立於 1996 年 3 月 27 日，是繼台灣電視公司 (台視)、中國電視公司 (中視) 以及中華電視公司 (華視) 之後，台灣的第四家無線電視台，同時也是台灣的第一家民營無線電視台。

解析

(D) 1. 本題問導致 2006 年國際海洋音樂祭延期的原因為何，線索在第一段第三句：...the rock festival had to be postponed because of Tropical Storm Bilis，因此答案選 (D) 熱帶風暴碧利斯。

(B) 2. "postponed" 意思為「被延遲」，因此答案選 (B) 後來才舉行；其他選項的意思如下：(A) 被取消；(C) 被首次演出；(D) 被很快完成。

(D) 3. 本題問有關今年 (2006) 國際海洋音樂祭的敘述何者為非，答案選 (D)，線索在第二段第五句：Totem, last year's winner, performed this year. 由本句可知圖騰樂團是去年的冠軍，當然也不會是新樂團之一。

(C) 4. 本題問 4 個選項中，哪一個不是今年 (2006) 音樂祭遭遇的問題，首先在第三段第二、三句可以找到對新主辦單位民視的抱怨：...complained that the new organizer made the festival into too much of a commercial event，因此 (D) 是對的；接著同樣在第三段的下一句，交通問題：traffic was in chaos，所以 (A) 也是對的；此外還有天氣問題，在第一段第三句：the rock festival had to be postponed because of Tropical Storm Bilis，因此答案選 (C) 各樂團間的競爭，從第二段第三、四句可以得知，這種競爭被視為是 the highlight of the festival，所以當然不會是問題之一。

（　A　）5. 本題問 4 個選項中的哪一個字意思代表 「導致短暫延誤的小問題」，答案選 (A)(細微的) 障礙；其他選項的意思如下：(B) 衝擊，影響；(C) 爭論，辯論；(D) 競爭。

Pop Quiz 解答

1. commercials　2. role　3. notable　4. impact　5. relax

翻　譯

2007 年 8 月

　　貓空曾是台北最廣闊的茶葉種植區，山巒疊翠，步道蜿蜒，加上靜謐的茶莊，讓它成了台灣體驗道地「茗茶文化」的絕佳去處。近來又有貓空纜車系統開始營運，對於有意到該景點一探究竟的觀光客而言，更是方便許多。

　　貓纜系統於 2007 年 7 月 4 日開始營運，起初大家都很興奮，因為纜車連接了台北捷運動物園站，如此一來到貓空就方便許多。纜車的人氣的確很高，開幕以來，搭乘人次已超過 40 萬，令人遺憾的是，在過去的一個多月中，系統上的諸多問題和事故揮之不去，導致原先對新纜車的興奮之情已漸轉為失望。

　　起初，民眾大排長龍迎接貓纜開幕，但因纜車沒有空調，內部溫度過高讓許多乘客抱怨連連；接著，營運才沒幾天，又因為雷擊造成系統關閉長達 5 個小時之久，讓數百名乘客受困在半空中；接下來幾個禮拜，纜車系統又因故障和設備失靈而多次關閉，有些人因而擔心纜車系統的安全性。

　　對於這些關切，台北市長郝龍斌向大眾再三保證搭乘纜車的安全性。台北市政府也已宣布，貓空纜車系統將於每週一關閉，以進行定期的安全檢查。

　　大家都希望這些問題和爭議都能盡快獲得解決，因為貓空無疑是個美麗的地方，而貓纜系統則提供觀光客一個既方便又賞心悅目的管道前來造訪。

補　充

1. **Maokong Gondola**　貓空纜車

　　簡稱貓纜，是台北市於 2007 年 7 月 4 日啟用之纜車系統，用以連接台北市立動物園與貓空地區，全線共 4 站，總長 4.03 公里。它是截至目前為止台灣最長，同時又具有大眾運輸性質的纜車，同時也是台北市首座觀光休憩用纜車。

2. **Hau Lung-bin**　郝龍斌

　　政治人物，1952 年 8 月 22 日生於台北市，是中華民國前行政院長、參謀總長郝柏村之子。2006 年他代表國民黨參選台北市長，在選戰中擊敗民進黨候選人謝長廷，以及獨立候選人宋楚瑜、柯賜海，順利當選。

3. **Taipei City Government**　台北市政府 (the～)

台北市最高行政機關，屬直轄市政府位階，隸屬於行政院管轄。組織架構方面，在市長、副市長以下設有 15 局、7 處、8 委員會，此外尚有台北市政府捷運工程局、自來水事業處等直屬機構，轄下編制員工總計約 7 萬餘人。

解 析

(D) 1. 本題答案為 (D)，線索在第一段第一句後半 "...one of the best places in Taiwan to experience authentic 'tea culture'" 以及第五段 "...Maokong is definitely a beautiful place..." 從以上形容可知，貓空在纜車啟用前，原本就屬觀光聖地，只不過纜車的啟用讓往返方便，以致觀光客數量更多而已。

(A) 2. 本題問 4 個選項中，哪一個不是貓空纜車啟用後曾遭遇過的問題，答案選 (A) 缺乏觀光客，線索在第三段第一句 "...long lines greeted the opening of the gondolas..." 可見觀光客很多；至於其他選項 (B) 設備失靈；(C) 車廂內高溫；以及 (D) 系統故障等都曾發生過。

(B) 3. 本題問在第二段中出現的單字 "plague"(使受災禍) 意思為何，從文中出現在 plague 之前的 "disappointment"、"a number of problems" 等線索可推測本字應具有負面意義，因此可剔除 (A)、(C) 兩個選項，(D) 選項意思是「散播疾病」，與全文敘述完全不相干，因此合理推測答案為 (B) 造成麻煩。

(D) 4. 本題問 4 個與貓纜系統相關的敘述中，哪一個是正確的。(A) 錯，線索在第四段第二句 "...Maokong Gondola system will be closed every Monday..."；(B) 錯，線索在第三段第一句 "...they did not have air conditioning..."；(C) 錯，線索在第二段第一句 "...began operation on July 4, 2007..." 因此營運至今尚不足 10 年；答案選 (D) 自貓纜開始營運後，一直有許多安全上的顧慮。

(C) 5. 本題問敘述錯誤的選項，答案選 (C)，線索在第一段第二句 "...with the opening of the new Maokong Gondola system, it has also become much more convenient for visitors to explore this scenic spot..." 根據本句可知，讓參訪貓空更為方便的，並非捷運的動物園站，而是貓空纜車。

Pop Quiz 解答

1. B　2. A　3. C　4. D　5. C

UNIT 18

翻譯

2005 年 8 月

在遭受連續自殺炸彈攻擊、一次企圖引爆炸彈未遂以及警方誤槍殺一位無辜平民後，倫敦持續陷入了緊張不安的氣氛中。

麻煩開始於 7 月 7 日。在這起倫敦有史以來最嚴重的自殺炸彈攻擊事件中，4 名自殺炸彈客在倫敦的大眾運輸系統引爆炸彈。其中 3 次爆炸發生於倫敦的地鐵系統，也就是地下鐵，還有一枚炸彈摧毀了一輛雙層巴士。總計有 56 人因此喪生，受傷者更多達數百名。

接著在 7 月 21 日，倫敦的運輸系統又受到另一次炸彈攻擊。這次的炸彈只有部份被引爆，因此無人喪生。然而，整個城市已經被這第二次的攻擊事件所撼動，因為它與第一次攻擊只相隔了兩個星期。

英國首相湯尼·布萊爾極力呼籲倫敦市民保持冷靜，不要讓攻擊事件擾亂了他們的日常生活。同時，警方也加速腳步追蹤可能的自殺炸彈嫌犯，並且制定了一套「射殺」政策。7 月 22 日，第二次炸彈攻擊隔天，警察在倫敦地鐵站裡槍殺了一名可疑的炸彈客。但警方後來才得知，這名巴西男子，瓊·查爾斯·梅尼士，是無辜的，他與炸彈攻擊案並沒有任何關連。

政府官員為這次的誤殺事件向全國人民道歉，但仍誓言會盡全力阻止今後在英國境內再次發生炸彈攻擊事件。目前已經有 11 個人因涉及 7 月 21 日的炸彈攻擊事件而被逮捕，然而，在有關 7 月 7 日的爆炸案調查方面，尚未有任何人遭到逮捕。警方仍試圖查明這兩起炸彈攻擊是否有關連。

補充

1. Tony Blair 湯尼·布萊爾

前英國首相，自 1994 年 7 月起出任英國工黨黨魁，期間破舊立新、大肆改革，結果在 1997 年大選中獲得壓倒性勝利。1997 至 2007 年間擔任首相，是工黨史上在任最久的一位，但最後由於種種批評，於 2007 年 6 月 27 日卸任。

2. Jean Charles de Menezes 瓊·查爾斯·梅尼士

巴西國民，在倫敦南部以電工為生，2005 年 7 月 22 日在史塔克維爾地鐵站遭便衣刑警槍殺，當時他被警方認定為自殺炸彈客，且正要進行一項恐怖攻擊，但事後卻證明他完全無辜。

3. **Brazil** [brə`zɪl] 巴西

南美洲最大國家，人口數及土地面積均居世界第五。憑藉豐富的天然資源以及充足的勞動力，其國內生產總值為南美第一；此外，由於曾遭葡萄牙殖民，現今之官方語言仍為葡萄牙語。

解 析

(C) 1. 從文章第二段可知，在 7 月 7 日發生的 4 起爆炸案中，有 3 起的攻擊目標是地鐵 (subway)，1 起攻擊雙層巴士 (double-decker bus)；而 7 月 21 日遭炸彈攻擊的地點也是運輸系統 (transit system)，文章中並未提到有大眾傳播媒體 (mass media) 遭到攻擊，因此答案選 (C)。

(D) 2. 文章第五段最後一句提到：The police are still trying to determine if there is any connection between the two attacks. 亦即警方尚無法證明 7 月 7 日與 7 月 21 日所發生的兩起恐怖攻擊相關，因此答案選 (D)。

(D) 3. 文章中的 "on edge" 被用於形容在經過數起炸彈攻擊，以及一次警方誤殺無辜民眾後，倫敦市的景況或氣氛，所以照常理推斷，應該是極為緊張或不安，答案選 (D)。

(B) 4. (A) 錯，Menezes 被殺是因為警方認定他是 suspected bomber，並非因為他來自巴西；(C) 錯，在事件後，警方並未承諾要停止 "shot-to-kill" 的政策，只是誓言要 continue their efforts to prevent future bombings；(D) 也錯，文章最後一段只提到官員為誤殺事件道歉，但並未提到有部分官員仍懷疑 Menezes 有罪；因此答案選 (B)。

(D) 5. (A) 錯，根據文章第三段第二句，在 21 日的炸彈攻擊中，由於 the bombs only partly detonated, 所以 no one was killed；(B) 錯，因為根據第四段第三句，Menezes 遇害是在 July 22，並非在 21 日爆炸發生後立刻被殺；(C) 也錯，第一段第一句提到在炸彈攻擊後，倫敦市陷入緊張不安的氣氛當中，但並未提到有市民決定離開。答案選 (D)，線索在第二段第二句。

Pop Quiz 解答

1. E 2. C 3. D 4. I 5. G

UNIT 19

翻 譯

2008 年 10 月

中國毒奶與有毒食品事件爆發以來，首當其衝的就是中國，接著台灣和亞洲其他地區也受到波及，而目前已在歐洲和北美引發問題，它引發全球性的恐慌，並讓許多人對其購買及食用物品的安全性產生懷疑。

今年年初問題開始出現在中國，當地發現有部分酪農在牛奶與奶粉中添加了一種工業用化學物質——三聚氰胺。三聚氰胺主要用於製造塑膠，但它也能添加於食品中，用以增加氮含量，使食品看似富含蛋白質。然而，食用過多的三聚氰胺可能會導致腎結石，接著是腎衰竭，最終造成死亡。

而這正是發生在中國的事情。據中國政府官員統計，光在九月，就有超過 53,000 名的嬰兒，在飲用遭三聚氰胺污染的嬰兒配方奶粉後發病，其中 4 位更因此喪命。這項消息自然讓中國許多地區的人民感到恐慌，尤其是曾讓小孩吃過嬰兒配方奶粉的父母，這些驚恐的父母火速將小孩送往各地醫院進行檢查。

在台灣，這項消息同樣引起關切。台灣衛生署目前雖然已經採取行動來處理問題，但部分人士仍批評衛生署及政府對危機處理的速度過慢。而在之後發現某些奶精同樣也受到三聚氰胺污染時，恐慌程度更是大幅提昇。

雖然中國官員聲稱目前問題已獲控制，但近來的報導所呈現的卻完全是另一回事。受污染的糖果在歐洲與美國陸續被發現，而中國製的餅乾和巧克力目前也正接受調查中。

不過，這次可怕的危機還是可能產生一些正面的結果。也許，這次的「食物恐慌」將催生對中國的食物與乳製品採取更嚴密的法規規範和監控。如此一來，各地的人民將可以再次對食品——特別是來自中國的食品——感到安心。

補 充

1. melamine [`mɛləmin] 三聚氰胺

俗稱密胺、蛋白精，被用作化工原料，是製造美耐皿樹脂的原料。該樹脂常用於製造日用器皿、裝飾貼面板、織物整理劑等。三聚氰胺對身體有害，不可用於食品加工或食品添加物。

2. **nitrogen** [ˋnaɪtrədʒən] 氮

氮是一種化學元素，通常的單質形態是氮氣，是無色無味無臭，十分不易有化學反應的原子的氣體，可以令火焰立刻熄滅。氮氣分佈在全地球，是地球大氣中最多的氣體，占大氣體積的 **78%**。

3. **Department of Health** 衛生署

隸屬於行政院，為國家衛生、醫療等全民健康事務之最高主管機關，其下設有醫事處、藥政處、食品衛生處、護理及健康照護處等處所，以及疾病管制局、中央健康保險局、管制藥品管理局等附屬機關。

解 析

(B) 1. 本題線索在文章最後一段第二句 ： ...this food scare will lead to tighter regulations...dairy products in China.，答案選 (B)。

(A) 2. 本題線索在第四段第二句 ： ...some have criticized the department...slow to react to this crisis.，因此 (A) 選項說：「台灣政府迅速處理此危機」是錯的。

(A) 3. 本題線索在第三段最後一句 ： Children were rushed by terrified parents to local hospitals for check-ups.，因此答案選 (A)。(B) 的線索在第五段第一句：Although officials in China say...a far different story. 由本句可知中國政府並未能控制其擴散，因此 (B) 不能選；(C) 的線索在下一句後半段：...cookies and chocolates...under investigation，亦即部分食品尚在調查中，結果當然尚未公佈，因此 (C) 不能選；(D) 選項雖然文章中並未直接提到，但根據第三段的敘述做合理推測，一般人應該不會再繼續購買含毒乳製品，因此 (D) 不能選。

(C) 4. (A) 是錯的，由第二段第三句：...making them appear to be rich in protein 可知，酪農添加三聚氫胺是為了讓食品看似富含蛋白質，而非增添美味；(B) 也錯，從第五段第一句：Although officials in China say...a far different story. 可知，中國政府並未吐實；第五段第二句表示，在歐洲及美國也發現了受污染的糖果，因此 (D) 是錯的：答案選 (C)。

(A) 5. 衛生署官員對食物進行調查的目的在於讓人們 once again start to feel secure about the things they consume（最後一段第三句），亦即「確認食物是否安全或符合品質標準」，答案選 (A)。

Pop Quiz 解答

1. A　2. C　3. B　4. D　5. C

2007 年 12 月

　　在過去，台灣的經濟是亞洲的驕傲，也是全世界其他國家羨慕的對象。多年來，台灣的經濟強勁且穩定成長，全島人民繁榮發展，台灣的中產階級也日益壯大。但是，近來情況卻有所改變。研究顯示，其實台灣目前的經濟已漸趨 M 型化，並持續往這個方向發展。

　　當經濟朝 M 型化發展時，會有許多低所得者，也會有許多高所得者，但平均所得者就不多了。所以基本上來說，目前台灣的有錢人比以往更多，可是台灣現今的窮人也變多了，而且台灣的中產階級一直在萎縮中。

　　此外，根據政府一項研究顯示，台灣最貧窮家庭的年平均所得，從 2000 年的台幣52,820 元，跌落至 2006 年的 34,866 元；另一方面，台灣最富有家庭的年平均所得則從 2000 年的 1,621,747 元，成長至 2006 年的 1,741,669 元。

　　對中產階級者而言，許多人都發現他們的工時變長，但賺的錢卻比過去更少。有些人在壓力之下要加班，但卻沒能因這些額外的工時而獲得加班費或任何其他利益。這些人有時被稱為「窮忙族」，他們的工作常屬於銷售、廣告，或是服務業，糟糕的是，認為自己屬於「窮忙族」的人與日俱增。

　　所以很明顯地，台灣的經濟在許多方面都正在改變中。不幸的是，當中有些改變並不好，因為台灣極貧與極富間的差距持續在擴大，而且愈來愈多的中產階級工時拉長，工資卻更少。

1. **M-shaped** [`ɛm `ʃept] M 型化的

　　M 型化為日本趨勢學家大前研一提出的概念，主要說明中產階級消失，貧富兩極化的現象。

2. **middle class** 中產階級

　　一般指經濟獨立，擁有固定工作的人士，他們屬於社會中的中堅份子，具穩定社會及促進其發展的力量。各國界定中產階級的因素不同，但大致以收入及資產判別，一般擁有私家車及自用住宅者，便可稱為中產階級。

(C) 1. 本題問的是 M 型化社會的結構，線索在第二段第一、二句：a lot of people with low incomes...a lot of people with high incomes...not many people with average incomes.，亦即偏向貧富兩極化，答案選 (C)。

(C) 2. 本題錯誤選項為 (C)，線索在第四段第一句：... middle class, ...are working longer hours, but are making less money... 因此說他們的年平均收入增加是錯誤的。

(D) 3. 本題問哪種職業的人不屬於「窮忙族」，線索在第四段第三句：... they often have jobs in sales, advertising, or the service industry. 選項 (A) 屬銷售行業，(B)、(C) 屬服務業，因此答案選 (D) 教師。

(B) 4. 本題問台灣中產階級對他們工作的想法，線索在第四段第一、二句：... many have discovered that they are working longer hours, but are making less money than they did in the past... 因此答案選 (B)。

(A) 5. 本題問台灣的經濟結構正在如何變化？線索在文章第三段，其中提到極貧家庭和極富家庭從 2000 年到 2006 年間的年收入變化，極貧者收入減少而極富者收入增加，因此 (A) 選項說兩者差距變大是正確的。

Pop Quiz 解答

1. households　2. prospered　3. steadily　4. average　5. wealthy

UNIT 21

台灣兒童愛喝汽水，不喝開水

翻 譯

2007 年 10 月

你喜歡喝汽水嗎？台灣的小孩肯定喜歡！最近一份報告揭露，有 45 % 的台灣兒童每天至少會飲用非酒精飲料一次，有許多人甚至每天不只喝一次。

這項調查是由名為兒童福利聯盟文教基金會（簡稱 CWLF）的非營利機構所進行，總計全台灣有超過 1,000 名四、五年級的學童接受調查，被問及有關他們「飲料習慣」的相關問題。

世界衛生組織的一項類似調查顯示，只有以色列兒童比台灣兒童飲用更多蘇打飲料。根據這項調查，美、英兩國的兒童在相較之下，喝的蘇打飲料就比台灣兒童來得少。

兒福聯盟的調查結果中有更多驚人的事實。除了汽水之外，許多台灣學童都承認，他們每天飲用含糖的茶飲、冷飲、甚至咖啡。令人震驚的是，百分之五的受訪學生更進一步表示，他們經常購買含酒精飲料。

此外，這項調查也顯示，台灣大多數小孩喝的水太少，台灣學童平均一天只喝 1,200 cc（立方公分）的白開水，其中 10 % 甚至只喝 500 cc，兩者都少於台灣政府建議的每日 1,500 cc 到 2,000 cc 的攝取量。

如果學生想確保他們飲用足量的水，依照兒福聯盟的說法，他們就該試著每天喝至少 6 杯白開水；此外，兒福聯盟表示，父母也能扮演督促小孩多喝水的角色，舉例來說，父母本身如果能喝開水，不喝非酒精飲料，就能成為孩子的好榜樣。

補 充

1. Child Welfare League Foundation (CWLF) 兒童福利聯盟文教基金會

兒童福利聯盟文教基金會為一公益性組織，自民國 80 年 12 月成立以來，一直致力於兒童福利工作的推展，其服務內容包括兒童相關法令政策的修訂與倡導、收出養服務、失蹤兒童協尋以及托育咨詢等。

2. World Health Organization 世界衛生組織

隸屬於聯合國之下，為國際最大的公共衛生組織，總部設於瑞士日內瓦。該組織之主要任務有三：促進流行病和地方病防治；提供並改進公共衛生、疾病醫療及相關教學與訓練；推動確定生物製品的國際標準。

3. Israel [ˈɪzrɪəl] 以色列

1948 年於西亞巴勒斯坦地區建國，目前人口數近 740 萬，主要為猶太人。首都為耶路撒冷，但外國使館大多設於特拉維夫。就中東地區而言，以色列在經濟、商業自由、新聞自由等方面，都被視為是發展程度最高的國家。

解 析

(C) 1. 選項 (A) 錯在台灣學童平均每天只喝 1,200 cc，而非 2,000 cc 的白開水（第五段第二句）；(B) 錯在台灣學童每天喝的水並不足量，他們應喝的量為 1,500 ～ 2,000 cc（第五段第三句）；(D) 錯在有 45%，而非 5% 的學童每天至少喝一次非酒精飲料（第一段第三句）；答案選 (C)，線索在第三段第一句。

(D) 2. 本題 (A) 不能選，因為全文僅陳述該組織執行了一項有關兒童飲料習慣的調查，並未提到亞洲童工問題；(B) 錯在台灣兒童喝的蘇打飲料比美國兒童多，而不是少（第三段第二句）；(C) 錯在建議兒童一天喝 1,500 ～ 2,000 cc 白開水的是台灣政府，而非兒福聯盟文教基金會（第五段第三句）；(D) 正確，線索在最後一段最後一句。

(A) 3. 本題線索在第五段最後一句：...Taiwanese government's recommendation of 1,500 to 2,000 cc of water consumption each day. 以及第六段第一句：...they should try to drink at least six glasses of plain water every day, according to the CWLF.，答案選 (A)。

(B) 4. 本題答案選 (B)，從第三段第一句：...only children in Israel drink more soda than children in Taiwan. 的敘述可知，以色列兒童喝的蘇打飲料就比台灣兒童喝的多。

(D) 5. 本題問文章主旨，文章第一段就點明在台灣有許多學童愛喝飲料，二、三段提到有兩個機構就台灣學童愛喝飲料的習慣各做了一項調查，第四段指出調查報告的部分結果，即台灣學童常喝的飲料種類，第五段說明台灣學童由於愛喝飲料，導致水的攝取量不足，最後一段則建議學童應攝取足量的水，並鼓勵父母以身作則。從以上各段摘要可明顯看出，本文主旨在說明台灣兒童愛喝飲料、不愛喝水的事實，故答案選 (D)。

Pop Quiz 解答

1. beverage   2. consumption   3. recommendations   4. Additionally
5. on a daily basis

UNIT 22

恐怖襲擊孟買

翻 譯

2009 年 1 月

2008 年 11 月 26 日開始，恐怖份子以一連串經過精密協調策劃的行動，攻擊位於印度孟買市中心的多處不同地點，數百人在市內各地喪生或遭挾持。而在突擊隊員猛攻泰姬瑪哈宮殿與塔樓飯店，並在一場激烈的戰役中殲滅最後一群恐怖份子後，這場長達三天的攻擊行動才終於宣告落幕。

大多數的暴力事件均發生於泰姬飯店，一個極受歡迎的觀光景點，而總計 10 名的恐怖份子同時也攻擊了孟買市內的其他多處地點，其中包含一處猶太中心，以及市內最大的火車站。根據印度政府的報告，總計有 173 人於槍擊及爆炸中喪生，308 人受傷。

政府官員表示，攻擊者搭船抵達，並迅速散佈至孟買市內各地；暴力事件似乎是隨機發生，而且攻擊者並非如先前報導所說，鎖定外國人為攻擊目標。警方在戰鬥中格殺了 10 名可疑份子中的 9 人，而唯一的生還者，名為埃吉蒙‧埃米爾‧卡薩布的 21 歲巴基斯坦男子，目前則仍遭警方拘留。

印度政府處理恐怖攻擊的能力立即遭受質疑。官員在 2007 年就曾收到過警告，表示恐怖份子計畫要從水路襲擊孟買，但維安部隊並沒有足夠的設備及武器來防止這類的大型攻擊。

證據指出，部分以巴基斯坦為基地的伊斯蘭團體，可能要為這次的孟買攻擊事件負責。在事件後數週，巴基斯坦政府逮捕了數名與該攻擊事件相關的成員。同時，巴基斯坦官員也計畫要與印度政府合作，採取行動以對抗恐怖活動。

自從恐怖攻擊後，印度各地便不斷在舉辦葬禮及各項紀念活動，而孟買也正奮力要回歸正常生活。

補 充

1. Mumbai [ˌmʌmˈbaɪ] 孟買

英國殖民時期舊稱為 Bombay，是印度第一大城兼馬哈拉施特拉邦首府，位於印度西南方，它同時也是印度金融貿易中心，以及電影娛樂工業「寶萊塢」(Bollywood) 的所在地。

2. Taj Mahal Palace and Tower Hotel 泰姬瑪哈宮殿與塔樓飯店

位於孟買市中心，是擁有 105 年歷史的著名豪華飯店。由於入住房客多為各國高官顯要或名人富豪，導致它在「2008 年 11 月孟買恐怖攻擊事件」中成為恐怖份子攻擊的主要目標。

3. **Jewish** [ˈdʒuɪʃ] *adj.* 猶太人 (教) 的

   Jew [dʒu] *n.* [C] 猶太人

   猶太人為信奉猶太教的中東地區古老民族，自 2000 多年前失去國家土地後，便開始在世界各地流浪，期間各種歧視及迫害不斷，尤以二次世界大戰中德國納粹的大屠殺為最；1948 年，猶太人終於得以在巴勒斯坦地區重建國家以色列，但同時也開啟了當地嚴重而漫長的種族衝突。

4. **Pakistani** [ˌpækɪˈstænɪ] *adj.* 巴基斯坦 (人) 的

   Pakistan [ˌpækɪˈstæn] 巴基斯坦

   巴基斯坦面積約 80 萬平方公里，人口 1 億 7 千多萬，是南亞的重要回教國家。1947 年與印度分裂並脫離英國統治而獨立，但是由於領土與宗教問題，與印度的衝突不斷。

5. **Islamic groups** 伊斯蘭團體

   此處的伊斯蘭團體指的是虔誠軍，1991 年該組織成立於阿富汗，目前的根據地則是在巴基斯坦境內的拉合爾附近。該組織成立的目的在於終結印度對喀什米爾地區的統治，曾多次在印度境內發動大規模的恐怖攻擊，目前英、美、印度、巴基斯坦等國都將其列為恐怖組織。

解 析

(B) 1. 本題線索在第一段的第一、三句，第一句提到 Terrorists attacked... in a series of coordinated strikes that began on November 26, 2008. ，而第三句說 The siege ended 3 days later when commandos...eliminated the last group of terrorists... ，從這兩個句子可知，恐怖攻擊始於 11 月 26 日，並於 3 天後結束，因此答案應選 (B) 11 月 29 日。

(D) 2. 本題線索在第二段。由第一句 Most of the violence occurred in the Taj hotel... 可知泰姬飯店為主要攻擊目標；而第二句 ...terrorists also attacked...other places...including a Jewish center and the largest train station in the city. 則指出恐怖份子攻擊的其他地點還有一處猶太中心以及孟買市內最大的火車站，因此 (A)、(B)、(C) 都對，答案選 (D) 泰姬瑪哈陵。

(B) 3. 本題線索在第三段第二句 The violence appeared to be random... 表示「暴力事件似乎是隨機發生的…」，也就是沒有特定的攻擊目標，因此答案選 (B)。

（ A ）4. 本題答案選 (A)，線索在第二段最後一句 ...173 people were killed...and 308 people were wounded. 亦即喪生者應為 173 人，而非 (A) 選項所說的 308 人；(B)、(C)、(D) 選項的敘述均正確，線索分別在第三段第一、二句、第五段第一句，以及第一段第三句。

（ D ）5. 選項 (A) 的前半段是對的，印度政府在 2007 年就曾收到過警告，但後半段說他們準備萬全是錯的，原因在第四段第二句 ...the security forces did not have enough equipment and weapons to prevent such a large attack.；(B) 錯在逮捕 Ajmal Amir Kasab 的並非巴基斯坦政府，理由則在於孟買為印度領地，在當地發生的攻擊事件當然是由當地警方或印度政府處理；(C) 則錯在印度政府並沒有足夠的武器來防止這類的大型恐怖攻擊，線索同樣在第四段第二句；(D) 選項正確，線索在第五段的最後一句。

Pop Quiz 解答

1. H   2. G   3. D   4. B   5. C

UNIT 23

洋基隊的台灣關係

翻　譯

2005 年 6 月

　　時間是春天的美好夜晚，地點在紐約市的洋基球場，再次爆滿的群眾正準備觀看紐約洋基隊出戰多倫多藍鳥隊。

　　不過今晚很不一樣。仔細觀察就能看出端倪，群眾中除了有中文的「加油」字樣，甚至還出現了中華民國的國旗。而站在投手丘上的是位來自台灣的高大投手——王建民。這位當紅的選手現年 25 歲，即將上演他在大聯盟的處女秀，而全世界都等著觀賞。

　　回到台灣當地，忠實的球迷，特別是王建民的台南鄉親們，對於他們心目中的英雄有著高度的期許。他們相信這位在 2004 年帶領台灣棒球隊邁向奧運的明星，在美國職棒大聯盟裡必定也會有同樣讓人驚豔的表現。

　　王建民果然沒讓台灣和紐約的球迷失望，他的表現搶眼，讓前 10 位他面對的打者出局，只被打出 6 支安打、失掉 2 分，雖然王建民在第 7 局退場，但最終洋基還是以 4 比 3 贏得這場比賽。

　　以如此亮眼的表現，王建民結束了他在紐約洋基隊的歷史性處女秀。雖然王建民這一晚先發上場而未能贏得勝投，但他的表現著實獲得高度的讚賞。實際上，洋基總教練喬・托瑞就表示，王建民是他這 9 年來見過最好的新人投手。

　　自首次上場以來，王建民就已經累積了 3 勝 2 負的驚人紀錄。以新人之姿就能有這麼令人印象深刻的開始，看來這位來自台灣的洋基球員在大聯盟的前途的確是一片光明。

補　充

1. **New York Yankees**　(棒球) 紐約洋基隊

在美國職棒大聯盟中，隸屬於美聯東區的球隊，創立於 1901 年，曾 39 度參與世界大賽，並贏得其中的 26 次冠軍。它是大聯盟中球員總薪資最高 (2009 年薪資約 2 億美元)，且每個守備位置皆有球員獲選登錄棒球名人堂的球隊。

2. **Yankee Stadium**　洋基球場

這裡指的是位於紐約布朗克斯區，美國職棒大聯盟紐約洋基隊的舊主場，啟用於 1923 年，是大聯盟中歷史第 3 悠久的球場，可容納 57,545 名觀眾。該球場已於 2008 年球季結束後被拆除，並被同樣位於布朗克斯區的新球場所取代。

3. **Toronto Blue Jays** (棒球) 多倫多藍鳥隊

在美國職棒大聯盟中，隸屬於美聯東區的球隊，創立於 1977 年。它的主場位於加拿大多倫多市，目前是大聯盟中唯一的加拿大隊伍，同時也是唯一贏過世界大賽的非美國隊伍，曾在 1992 及 1993 兩度贏得世界大賽冠軍。

4. **Major League Baseball** (美國職棒) 大聯盟

創立於 1903 年，由美國聯盟 (14 支隊伍) 與國家聯盟 (16 支隊伍) 所組成。每支球隊都必須在季賽中打滿 162 場比賽，之後 2 個聯盟各產生 4 支隊伍打進季後賽，在季後賽決定聯盟冠軍後，再由 2 支聯盟冠軍隊打世界大賽。

解 析

(A) 1. 文章第一段第一句就說明了這場比賽的地點，是 ...at Yankee Stadium in New York City...，因此答案選 (A)。

(C) 2. 選項 (A) 錯在王建民為洋基隊，而非藍鳥隊投手，明顯的線索在第五段第一句：...Wang Chien-ming's historic debut as a New York Yankee...；(B) 錯在 2004 年奧運王建民率領的是台灣球隊，而非美國球隊，線索在第三段第二句：...Wang, ...who led Taiwan's baseball team to the Olympics in 2004...；本文描述王建民在大聯盟中的初賽，而由第三段第二句可知，這場比賽是在 2004 年的雅典奧運之後，因此 (D) 選項說王建民在大聯盟打球已經超過 20 年很明顯是錯的；答案選 (C)，線索在第五段最後一句。

(B) 3. 從第二段第四句可知，王建民在大聯盟初登場時應該是 25 歲，而非 24 歲，因此 (A) 是錯的；第三段第二句提到，王建民曾帶領中華棒球隊參加 2004 年奧運，由此可合理推測，王建民一定在台灣打過棒球，所以 (C) 也是錯的；(D) 的線索在第四段第三句：...Wang leaves the game in the seventh inning...，由本句可知王建民並沒有投完整場比賽；答案選 (B)。

(D) 4. 本題線索在第四段第三句後半：...the Yankees go on to win the game four to three...，亦即洋基隊最後以 4 比 3 的比數贏得比賽，答案選 (D)。

(B) 5. 第四段第一句的敘述：Fans in Taiwan and New York are not disappointed as Wang puts in a strong performance. 與選項 (B) 所說，王建民的表現讓紐約與台灣球迷失望的敘述剛好相反，因此答案選 (B)。

Pop Quiz 解答

1. A 2. C 3. B 4. D 5. B

UNIT 24

美國校園再傳悲劇

翻 譯

2007 年 5 月

美國發生其近代歷史上最慘重的掃射濫殺事件之後，有關殺手與事發當天的最新情況陸續傳出。

4 月 16 日星期一，維吉尼亞理工學院的 27 名學生和 5 位老師遭到持槍男子趙承熙射殺身亡。而趙承熙，這位 23 歲在該校主修英語的學生，最後也自我了斷，使得當天在該校喪生的人數達到 33 人。

調查人員指出，這樁暴行起始於當天早上，趙承熙闖進一棟宿舍，殺害了一名女學生以及舍監；接著，他前往郵局，將一個包裹寄給美國國家廣播公司 (NBC) 新聞網。數小時後，趙承熙闖入諾里斯大樓，他先用鏈子將所有門鎖死，然後依序走進每一間教室，射殺學生和老師。專家表示，趙承熙在 9 分鐘內開了 170 多槍，最後才舉槍射擊自己的頭部自盡。

在趙承熙寄給新聞台的包裹中，包含了一些照片和影片，這些東西對於他大開殺戒的動機透露了些許訊息。在影片中，趙承熙表達了他對校內富家子弟的憎惡，此外，他還讚揚「科倫拜校園事件」中的凶手。

不過，很多人仍然想知道，是什麼原因促使一個人犯下如此可怕的罪行。大多數人都形容趙承熙是個「獨行俠」；家族成員則說他一直是個沈默寡言的孩子，且說話時很少用完整的句子，因此，他在學校裡常被欺壓。就讀維吉尼亞理工學院期間，他也曾因心理疾病接受治療。

也許這場殺戮的真正原因永遠不會水落石出，然而專家將繼續調查此案，以了解發生的原因，希望避免此類悲劇再次重演。

補 充

1. **Virginia Tech** 維吉尼亞理工學院

   創立於 1872 年，地點位於維吉尼亞州西南部的黑堡鎮，是一所以工科為主的綜合性公立大學，在卡內基教育基金會的分類中，它屬於特高研究型大學。

2. **Cho Seung-hui** 趙承熙

   1984 年 1 月 18 日出生於南韓首爾，8 歲時隨父母移民美國。2007 年 4 月 16 日，他在維吉尼亞理工大學宿舍中與人爭吵後，以事先購買的手槍射殺 32 人、射傷 25 人後舉槍自盡。當時他是該校 4 年級生，主修英文。

3. **NBC News** 美國國家廣播公司新聞網

美國國家廣播公司 (National Broadcasting Company) 為美國三大電視網之一，同時也是傳媒聯合企業 NBC Universal 的一部份，總部位於紐約的洛克菲勒中心，它為美國 200 多家電視台提供節目，NBC News 為其分支之一。

4. **Columbine High School** 科倫拜高中

位於美國科羅拉多州傑佛遜郡的一所高中，在 1999 年 4 月 20 日曾發生過校園槍擊事件，當時兩名青少年學生——艾瑞克・哈理斯以及迪倫・克萊伯德——以槍械及爆裂物在校園中殺害 13 人、並造成其他 24 人受傷後自殺身亡。

解 析

(B) 1. 本題線索在第二段第一句：...twenty-seven students and five teachers... were shot and killed...，因此總數應該是 27 + 5 = 32 人；第二段最後一句的數目 33 指的是包含自殺兇手在內的死亡總人數。答案選 (B)。

(C) 2. 本題線索在第三段第一句：...the rampage began that morning when Cho entered a dormitory and killed a female student and a dorm supervisor... 因此答案選 (C)。

(B) 3. 本題線索在第四段第一、二句，其中提到在趙承熙寄給 NBC News 的包裹中，有部分影像可能與他的殺人動機有關：In the videos, Cho expressed his hate for the "rich kids" at Virginia Tech...，因此答案選 (B)。

(A) 4. 本題選錯誤選項，線索在第五段：第二句說他在大部分人眼中是個獨行俠，家人則說他是個安靜的孩子，第三句則說他在學校常被欺負，這些說法都與選項 (A) 的敘述相反，因此答案為 (A)。

(D) 5. 本題考文章主旨，第一段點明在美國史上最嚴重的校園槍擊案落幕後，事發經過及兇手身份等細節終於逐漸顯露，第二段簡單介紹兇手並說明在這次槍擊案中的死亡人數，第三段說明槍擊案的發生經過，第四段推測可能的行兇動機，第五段陳述兇手在別人眼中的形象，第六段結論表示事件仍將繼續調查，以避免類似案件再度發生。從以上敘述可知，本文主旨在探討這件美國史上最慘烈的校園槍擊案，因此答案選 (D)。

Pop Quiz 解答

1. G　2. C　3. A　4. F　5. E

UNIT 25

翻譯

2006 年 7 月

　　今年 6、7 月間，一場特殊的「熱病」侵襲全球，它的症狀之一便是對足球產生極大的興趣。染上這種病的人常常為了看足球賽而熬夜，有些人甚至會到街上歡呼跳舞，特別是當他們喜愛的球員進球，或是支持的隊伍贏球時。沒錯，這種特殊的熱病就是世足熱，每隔 4 年，它就會隨著世界盃足球賽的開打而發作。

　　今年的世界盃由德國主辦，賽會 32 支隊伍的球迷和支持者湧入該國，即便是無票的群眾，也能在公共廣場的電視牆觀看比賽過過乾癮，為各自支持的隊伍加油。

　　台灣的世足熱也十分瘋狂。世足賽事通常於夜間 11 點開始現場直播，部分賽事甚至要到凌晨 3 點才開打，但是酒吧及餐館即使在這麼晚的時間，依舊擠滿了加油的球迷。

　　隨著世界各地的人們在各項賽事結果、以及預測冠軍隊伍上下注，世足賽的賭盤也跟著達到最高峰。在賽事初期許多人都看好前冠軍巴西隊，也有不少賭客把賭注押在英國隊身上。因此，當這些隊伍被淘汰時，下注在這些隊伍上的人往往既震驚又苦惱。

　　雖然今年的世足熱已經告一段落，但請先做好準備，因為 2010 年世足熱肯定會再次襲捲全球！

補充

1. **World Cup** 世界盃

　 又名「世界盃足球賽」或「世界足球錦標賽」，是世界足壇水準最高、規模也最大的賽事，首屆賽事於 1930 年舉辦，之後每 4 年舉辦一次；世界盃決賽是全世界最受歡迎的賽事，2006 年全球約有 7.15 億觀眾收看其轉播。

2. **Germany** [ˋdʒɚmənɪ] 德國

　 德意志聯邦共和國的簡稱，位於歐洲中部，首都柏林。它是歐盟的創始會員國之一、聯合國及北大西洋公約組織的一員，也是世界第 4 大經濟體，在諸多科技領域上更是居於領先地位，人口超過 8,200 萬，為世界強國之一。

3. **Brazil** [brəˋzɪl] 巴西

　 足球王國。據統計，巴西全國有超過 2 萬支足球隊；此外，它的國家代表隊是唯一從 1930 至 2006 年為止，從未在世界盃足球賽中缺席的球隊，同時也是唯一曾 5 次奪得

世界盃冠軍的球隊。(有關巴西其他資料請參考 Unit 18 的補充)

解 析

(A) 1. 本題問何者不是世足熱的「症狀」之一，(B) 的線索在第一段第二句後半；(C) 的線索在第二段第一句；而在第一段第三句也可以找到與 (D) 選項符合的敘述；全文未出現與 coach (教練) 相關的敘述，因此答案選 (A)。

(D) 2. (A) 不能選，因為當自己支持的球隊輸球時，球迷的反應是 shocked and upset (第四段最後一句)，而非跟別人打架；(B) 錯在即使沒買到票，他們也會聚在公共廣場的電視牆前觀看比賽 (第二段第二句)；(C) 錯在有些人會在自己最愛的球員得分，或自己國家的球隊贏球時上街歡呼或甚至跳舞 (第一段第三句)，而非害羞的不敢表達；因此本題答案選 (D)，線索在第二段第二句。

(C) 3. 本題問作者描述世界盃狂熱時的語氣，從人們會熬夜看電視 (第一段第二句)、上街為自己喜愛的球員或隊伍歡呼 (第一段第三句)、沒買到票也會在廣場上看電視牆、以及酒吧和餐廳即使到了深夜，依然擠滿為世足賽加油的人潮 (第三段第二句) 等等敘述可以看出，作者描述的語氣是 (C) 興奮的。

(C) 4. 本題問文章第四段中的單字 "pitch" 意思為何？從前文 "reached a fever..." (達到狂熱的…) 以及後文中 "people all over the world bet on the outcome of the matches..." (全世界的人都在比賽結果上下注) 等等敘述可以推斷，"pitch" 應該是「高峰；頂點」的意思，因此答案選 (C)。

(D) 5. 第四段提到，全世界都有人針對世界盃比賽結果及預測冠軍隊伍下注，其中巴西和英國尤其熱門，因此當這兩支隊伍遭到淘汰時，將賭注押在這兩隊上，也就是輸錢的人，自然會感到 shocked and upset，故答案選 (D)。

Pop Quiz 解答

1. B　2. C　3. D　4. A　5. C

Vocabulary Index

單字索引

Answer Key

閱讀測驗與Pop Quiz解答

01. CADCB
02. DBBAC
03. CCBAA
04. CACBA
05. ABDAC
06. CBBCA
07. BDCBD
08. DDCAB
09. CDDCC
10. DAABA
11. CCDDC
12. CAABD
13. BCDCD
14. CBACD
15. BBBDA
16. DBDCA
17. DABDC
18. CDDBD
19. BAACA
20. CCDBA
21. CDABD
22. BDBAD
23. ACBDB
24. BCBAD
25. ADCCD

Pop Quiz

01. DBCCA
02. DGAEH
03. disasters, cyclones, As a result, devastation, In addition, victims
04. CDBBA
05. BCCAD
06. variety, fierce, at least, committed, meanwhile
07. FDGIB
08. DFAIBC
09. CDBAB
10. ACBDC
11. technology, communication, debuted, controversial, upset
12. CCADB
13. BDCCA
14. DADBC
15. BACCD
16. commercials, role, notable, impact, relax
17. BACDC
18. ECDIG
19. ACBDC
20. households, prospered, steadily, average, wealthy
21. beverage, consumption, recommendations, Additionally, on a daily basis
22. HGDBC
23. ACBDB
24. GCAFE
25. BCDAC

The Best Guide to Cloze Test for CEE
無敵文意選填王

郭慧敏／著

就是這一本！讓你徹底征服文意選填！
稱霸考場　無人能敵

1. 理論篇以實際考題為例，精闢分析解題步驟，讓您輕鬆掌握答題關鍵。
2. 實戰篇囊括歷屆大考試題，讓您藉由充分練習徹底熟悉出題模式。
3. 隨書附贈完整文章翻譯及詳實解題技巧，讓您迅速理解文章內容、有效增強解題能力。

The Best Guide to Reading Comprehension for CEE
無敵閱讀測驗王

郭慧敏／著

就是這一本！讓你徹底征服閱讀測驗！
稱霸考場　無人能敵

1. 理論分析篇為您精闢分析大考閱測文章及題目類型，教您如何在最短時間內掌握文章重點、選出正確答案。
2. 實戰演練篇涵蓋歷屆指考、學測及模考試題，讓您透過充分練習找出自己的盲點，克服閱讀測驗的障礙。
3. 解析篇包含文章完整翻譯及題目類型分析，並為您剖析答題關鍵所在，讓您完全掌握閱讀測驗之精髓。

新聞宅急通A、C

三民英語編輯小組　彙編

新聞＋英文＋閱讀測驗＋字彙
通通宅配到府

- 蒐羅近年來國內外重大新聞，由專業外籍作者撰寫道地文章，內容多元、題材新穎，讓你讀新聞學英文，安居自「宅」也能放眼國際。
- 歸納關鍵單字與片語，讓你完全掌握新聞要點、「急」速累積大量字彙；精心設計的閱讀測驗與字彙評量，更能立即診斷學習成效。
- 詳盡中譯及精闢解析，助你洞悉文章脈絡、強化理解能力；適時補充相關資料，讓你全盤「通」曉新聞的來龍去脈。